Mind Under Troubled Waters

SARAH CARMELE MCGRIFF

DEDICATION

I'd like to dedicate this book to the Most High. I am forever grateful and blessed to Him for creating me to bless this world with His talents He has bestowed in my Spirit. To my two other reasons for existing, **Antuan Jr.** and **Zyonn Makayla. God** knew what He was doing when He entrusted me to be your mother. I can only pray and wish for you both to fulfill the path that **God** has in store for you; my beautiful children. To my parents, **Fred** and **Emma**- I couldn't ask for better people to facilitate me into this world. Your love and everlasting support has been and will always be appreciated. Thank you so much for your endurance.

To my sisters, **Adrienne, Kaycee, Nicki, Lena,** and **Curtisha** I love you beautiful ladies beyond words- keep pushing. To all of my nieces, nephews, aunts, uncles and cousins- thank you so much for your love and support over the years. I hope I have done all of you proud.

To my ladies for life- **Jennifer, Deshawn, Nora, Renee,** and **Shantee;** you all are Queens and I am grateful to **God** for placing you all in my life. I pray that our friendship will continue to last for all time. To my fellow nursing friends and co-workers; our career may be tiring, emotional, and thankless, but the love and compassion we possess for our patients is everlasting and more rewarding than any price tag.

I will forever be grateful for Ms. **Odessa G. White** for taking a chance on me when I was unsure myself if I wanted to complete this book. Thanks for the conversations, the encouragement, and the drive you instilled in me to fulfill my dreams.

And lastly, to the beautiful soul who thought it was not robbery to read the first few chapters of my book. Thank you for your truthfulness; you are indeed a blessing from God. May you continue to smile through the storms of life; remain humble in times of trouble, and God will give you the desires of your heart. Love to you reading this book and too everyone in my life always- *SCM*.

PROLOGUE

"Mrs. Jenkins! Mrs. Jenkins!" The stout, balding cemetery caretaker reached over and carefully placed his hand on the shoulder of the grieving mother as she knelt beside her son's sky blue casket. The casket was the same color of his 1965 Chevrolet Impala. As she gazed at the flowers adorning the casket; Della Jenkins slowly lifted her bowed head and turned to look at the caretaker, tears of pain and confusion streaming down her face.. *"Okay Paul, I'm ready, but I'm not ready."* She placed her arms around his arm as Paul begin to lift her from her knees she faltered. Paul quickly helped her to a nearby chair, the same desolate chair she sat in thirty minutes ago gazing at her son's final resting place. The words of the minister drifted in and out of her

subconscious state. Paul motioned to one of the workers for a bottle of water and a cool washcloth. As Della sipped the water Paul wiped her forehead and neck, attempting to console a pain that was inconsolable. Finally regaining her composure, Della stood up and slowly walked to the Cadillac CTS that patiently waited for her to grieve Big T's sudden death.

As Paul helped her into the rear of the car, the chauffeur handed her a faded blue handkerchief. It was the same handkerchief that her mother-in-law made for Big T when he was baptized sixteen years ago. Big T never let that blue handkerchief out of his sight. Della wanted to keep it instead of burying it with her son, much to the dismay of her mother-in-law and husband. As she sat in the car, her grief suddenly turned to anger, hatred, and uncontrollable rage. She never knew... she was never told. The secrets, the lies, the deceit, the absolute betrayal of her soon-to-be estranged husband and his family. The history behind her son's death, apparently predetermined by the demons of his ancestors' past. As the CTS drove away, Della buried her face in her hands and continued to sob incessantly.

CHAPTER 1

Thomas 'Big T' Jenkins runs down the hallway, knocking over the table that sat violet orchids. He nearly trips on his own feet as he rushes his brother's room. "*Manny, Manny, it's time!*" Manny cocks his head at his oldest brother, giving him a look of disappointment, as if he already knows exactly what he means. "*Come on man, time to take a bath. I got things to do, people to see!*", Thomas shouts. As he prepares to scoop up his small frail brother, Manny begins to wail and thrash. Thomas sets him on his racer car bed and gives him a comforting hug. Manny reaches behind his brother, grabs his communication board, and writes on the board No, No, No three times. Thomas looks at the board, giving Manny a look of defeat. "*If you let me give you a bath, I will take you to Frieda's for some rainbow ice cream.*" Once again, Manny, knowing how to get to the epicenter of the kindness of his brother's heart returned the deal with a smile of approval.

Manny and Thomas walk out the door and race towards Thomas' 1965 Chevrolet Impala. "*Big T, where are you taking Manny?*" Thomas suddenly turns around, only to see his tall, slender father with skin as smooth and dark as cocoa, sitting under the shady oak tree, taking a puff of his pipe. The smile on Thomas' face slowly fades away- "*I-I-I'm taking Manny with me to get some ice cream, then we're going to Bumble's house, d-d-d dad*", Thomas stammers. As Manny lowers his head on his brother's shoulder, Robert Jenkins motions for his sons to come closer to him. "*You make sure he gets back here within the hour, his tutor is coming. And don't be too long at Freida's place and Bumble's house. I need to have a conversation with you about the upcoming school year.*" "*Yes sir*", Big T says and turns away and hurriedly walks to his car. He secures his brother on the passenger side, gets in, and revs the car up. He slowly backs out of the driveway, giving his dad a wave. Robert nods back as Big T pulls away. *"I fucking hate his demonic ass!"* Big T shouts glancing over at his little brother. Manny looks at his brother with sad eyes, and nods his head.

CHAPTER 2

Freida's Ice Cream and Treats has been a staple in the community of Dover since 1941. Three generations operate the historic location, being the first Jamaican-American business to open. From its humble beginnings in the back of a dilapidated barber shop to an immaculate storefront in the heart and soul of Kimbrough Street, the environment of the parlor is nothing but love and adoration for the hard working citizens in the black community on Dover's south side. Many things have occurred here; from the civil rights movement, where many black intellectuals and freedom fighters gathered to eat and discuss the events of the time; to the opening of the recreational center behind the parlor, Freida's has always been the place that served as a united front for equality and justice. Many local and national influential African-American leaders have made their rounds and planted their roots on Kimbrough Street. As Thomas carries his little brother on his shoulders into the ice cream parlor, he is greeted by many of his high school friends. Jarvis "Bumble" Harvey, Thomas' childhood friend and classmate, runs up to Thomas and grabs Manny off of his shoulders, giving him a playful spin before putting him down. "*Bumble, I thought I was gonna meet you at your house?*" "*T*", Bumble said, "*I had to get away from my stepmom.*" *She was trippin' to me about the damn dishes that weren't washed this morning; hell, it wasn't even my turn to wash the dishes. I had already washed the dishes yesterday, and the day before, and the day before. My sisters can wash the dishes too, but my dad doesn't make them do nothin'. I just can't stand being around her. My father thinks she's the best thing ever*". Thomas shakes his head as he approaches the counter to order Manny's favorite ice cream; Frieda's Rainbow

Cake, and a banana split for himself. *"Big T you are blessed to have great parents, especially your mom"*, said Bumble. *"I miss my mom every second, minute, day, week, month, and year* (Bumble's mother passed away six years earlier from cancer). *"Yeah I know,"* said T, *" but my dad trips all the time, pushing me to work out constantly for the NBA, stressing me about focusing on being an athlete. And my mom! She just stays silent, never stands up for me and Manny, and doesn't stand up to my overbearing dad. Bumble, look at how many great athletes that have been at our school, only to end up working low paying, worthless jobs or selling drugs. Them white folks at the school don't give a damn about us niggas! They only concerned about getting 'their own kind' the scholarships and recognitions. Recruiters don't even come to Middleton High School much to get athletes to commit to their schools. My dad only made it to college and the NBA for a short while because his godfather was a top recruiter at Baylor. I'm*

tired of him trying to push his dreams on me. I want

something more better, meaningful for my life and my

future." Bumble gave Thomas a look of disgust. *"Nigga,*

do you know how many people would kill to be in your

position right now? You have tons of recruiters coming

to you every day. Didn't you just come from University

of Tennessee last week with Jackson Byrnes? Damn T,

Tennessee has one of the top men's basketball

programs out now, with NBA scouts looking for players

all the time. And you telling me you want something

more meaningful in your life? Get the fuck out with

that! Getting' out the slums, bringing your family out

the hood, putting Dover on the map once and for all; the

community, the number of kids that look up to you and

want to be like you, not to mention making millions of

dollars with contracts, that's what needs to be

meaningful to you right now. I'm not saying that

getting a degree is important, but it's not the only thing. Besides, having a college degree doesn't necessarily guarantee a great job once you finish school. Look at the number of new college graduates with degrees and they can't even find jobs nor pay off that student loan debt." Thomas shot back- *"Playing in the NBA isn't guaranteed either! Just look at my sorry ass excuse for a father! Only played four seasons before he tore his ACL; ending his career. Became an alcoholic, always blaming everyone but himself for his problems and his pathetic life. Pressuring me to do all of these great things he didn't get a chance to do. Doesn't even care about Manny nor getting him the proper care he needs for his autism. Just sits around and 'prays the autism away'. Spends more time in that cult called Free Hope Missionary Baptist, listening and giving away the money he has to Rev. Jerkey, who don't give a shit about him nor the people in his congregation! I'm tired of it!*

The church is supposed to help the community not suppress it. I have not seen anything good come out of our church!'" "His name is Rev. Jackson, not Jerkey", snarled Bumble, *"and he has done more for the black community here than them white folks at City Hall and definitely more than your black ass have done! And besides, you have a good father. He may not hold the Father of the Year Award, but at least he is present in your life. My dad just walks around the house drinking, forever frozen in a drunken stupor since my mom passed away. I know he is grieving, but me and my sisters are hurting too. We need him, and he is too damn drunk to even take care of us let alone himself."* *"Well",* said Thomas, *"The way my father treats us, I wish he would stay drunk all the time. He just don't know when to quit, when to loosen up, when to stop- and I mean, STOP! I get tired of his constant bickering, negativity, and depressing bullshit about my brother, about me, about some dude named Pilo that he talks about all the time"*. "*Who the hell is Pilo?*"", asked Bumble. " *Man, I don't even know*", sighed Thomas, "*but my dad seems to blame all of his failures on him.*" As Thomas and Bumble talk in walks Jasmin Shanell, a childhood friend of theirs. She makes her way to the counter to order Freida's Monster Burger meal. She gives Manny a hug and kiss on the cheek. "*You still want to marry me one day, Manny*"? Jasmin smiles as she gives Thomas a big squeeze. Manny shows the brightest smile, only for it to be dimmed by Bumble. "*Girl, Manny don't want your skinny butt! He wants a thick girl with a big booty, big titties, long, fake hair, and-*". "*Bumble, damn man shut up, please!*", Thomas screams. "*My brother don't need to be hearing that mess!*" "*You shut up fool*", says Bumble. " *I mean damn, it ain't like Manny understands what the hell I'm saying anyways! He don't even talk for God's sake*"!

"Jarvis, you are the most ignorant and ill-informed human being I've ever had the displeasure of knowing!", yelled Jasmin Shanell. *"Just because Manny doesn't talk doesn't mean he doesn't know what's going on. You have no clue about autism and people who suffer from it. Read a dang book sometime and educate yourself"*. Thomas nodded in agreement, grabbed his brother's hand, and walked towards the door. *"Yeah, what Jasmin said!"*, said Thomas. *"You sound just like my damn dad- educate yourself!"*. As Thomas and Manny walk out the door, Jasmin gives Bumble a menacing look of disgust, and runs after him. As they get to Thomas' car, Thomas puts his brother in the back seat, straps on his seat belt, closes the door, and turns to Jasmin. *"Thank you so much for defending me and Manny in there. Sometimes, I don't even know why I bother with Bumble"*. *"It's okay Thomas"*, said Jasmin. *"Jarvis is a good guy, but he has so many issues within*

himself, especially dealing with the death of his mother. He has good intentions, he just doesn't express himself eloquently. To be honest, I don't think he knows how to". Thomas thought about all of the trouble Bumble has been getting himself into over the years and decided he needed to be more of a supportive system to Bumble. "I'll talk to him", said Thomas. "He is a good guy, but something is going on his head, and he needs to learn how to deal with his issues. He many even need to seek some counseling". "Speaking of counseling", said Jasmin. " I heard you need to get your required volunteer hours needed to wear the Silver Cord Honor when you graduate. I still mentor at Save Our Youth Community Center, and they can really use young black men, especially teenagers and school athletes, to mentor the young boys there. Sounds good?" "Hell yeah, that's a great idea", said Thomas. "I can take Manny with me to get him away from my overbearing father and really *teach those boys about life. His home school teacher is also there from time to time so he can get involved in the activities she has for the children there with disabilities*". Thomas climbs into the car and drives off. The thought of going back home to his egotistical father brought him a sense of hopelessness, but he now knows what he must do to get up from under the overbearing father and his passive mother. He looks in the rearview mirror at Manny, eating his ice cream, wishing he could have the innocence that his brother possess.

CHAPTER 3

"*Aaaaugh*! *Aaaugh*! *Somebody please help me*! *Please, please, please help me*"! Myrtice and Jacob rush down the dimly lit hallway to room 472. Jacob fumbles with the keys, struggling to unlock the door. "*Dammit Jacob, hurry up*!", yells Myrtice. "*I don't know why we are rushing anyways, there is nothing wrong with this crazy nut*! *Watch what I tell you*", snorted Jacob. "*I don't care if there's nothing wrong or not with her, you know what happened the last time the staff was slow to respond to Dawn, Licorice, or Flaming Felicia, whatever the hell she calls herself*", said the exasperated nurse to her young, naïve orderly. Jacob opens the door to a middle-aged extremely pale, Caucasian woman with disheveled red, curly hair. Her white hospital gown was dingy and her knees were black from her being on the floor. She frantically waves and motions for the staff to come in her room. *"Lookey here, you scalawags"*, says the demented patient. As she continually motions for the staff to come closer, she slowly turns her back against them. Suddenly, she bends over, exposing her soiled underside, and tells them to get a whiff. Jacob gags, gripping his stomach and rushes out into the hallway, as Myrtice stands with her hands on her hips, shaking her head. *"Clean up crew! It's that time again"*!, Myrtice yells down the hall. Three patient care assistants, as well as two other orderlies, rush into her room. They are gowned up, and as they quickly wrap her up in a sheet and carry her out of her room down to the showers, she cries, kicks, and screams for the Jetsons and Captain Kirk to beam her up into outer space. Myrtice walks by Jacob, still trying keep his insides from coming up. *"Suck it up, Jacob, go to room 477, and check on you- know-who"*. Jacob suddenly hops to his feet, and gives Myrtice a look of despair.

"Dang Myrtice, how come you never go check on him? Because I'm the nurse, and I give the orders around here. Apply yourself with an education, and you can grow up to be like me one day", snarled the elderly, overweight, Caucasian woman. *"Like you? You mean miserable, single, and sexless?"* Jacob shot her a dirty look and walked away. He hated her with a passion but he knew he had to keep working at the hellhole known as Healing Minds Mental Institute until he was able to save up money to start his own dog breeding business. As he came close to room 477, he stood there for a few minutes, thinking about the patient that inhabited the space. The patient was eccentric in every sense of the word. He never talked, and the medical staff deemed him unsafe to be around others. He's had numerous, violent outbursts in the past, which resulted in tragic results. What those results were? Jacob didn't quite know, for it was before his time. For the few months

Jacob has been here he's never seen any visitors for the patient in room 477. No phone calls, no letters, no gifts, not even any knowledge of his family. His chart was kept away from most staff, including him. As a matter of fact, when Jacob first started, he and the other new employees were warned not to even discuss the patient in room 477 under any circumstances, unless they wanted to be terminated. They were to give the bare, and absolute bare, personal care to him. They were not to communicate with him at all. He was given a menu to choose his daily meals, and if he didn't circle anything (which most of the time he didn't), the kitchen just fixed whatever they felt like giving him. It doesn't take much for him to go off the deep end and many staff members don't like to deal with him. Jacob, however, has taking somewhat of a liking to him. He was intrigued by the mysterious aura of the reclusive patient. The more the staff was reminded to stay away from the patient, the more Jacob was curious to know about him. Jacob knocked on the door- *"Hey man, it's me, Jacob. I'm coming in to check on ya' and get your dinner order"*. For a moment, there is silence as Jacob waits to open the door. He puts the key in the hole, turns, and slowly opens the door. He quietly walks into a cold, spiritless box that is padded from wall to wall to floor. The mattress thrown against the corner of the room is in terrible shape, with the stuffing falling out. No sheets were given to him, he has a worn-out brown blanket, and a pillow with no pillow case. The bed frame is completely uninhabitable. The patient sits on the padded floor, reading a hip-hop magazine that is years old and not even in print anymore. Damn, at least these sorry ass maintenance crew can get this man a new bed, thought Jacob as he began to have pity on the poor soul. The patient stood up, coming into full view of the nervous orderly. He stood six feet, five inches tall to be exact, skin the color of caramel, and sporting a short, brown afro. His gold-wire framed glasses sits atop his forehead; and the light blue hospital gown swallows him. The pathetic medical staff won't even give him a smaller gown that is in better shape than the one he has on. He turns his back on Jacob, picking up a piece of paper and a black crayon. He gives Jacob the menu. As usual, the patient didn't circle anything for dinner but Jacob did notice something written in black on the back of the menu. *"Grilled turkey and cheese sandwich, no crust, tomato soup, grapes, two Dr. Peppers, and ice. And can I finally get some damn ice that's not halfway melted, please!"*, Jacob read aloud. He lets out a big chuckle. The patient nods his head and lets out a chuckle of his own. *"Be right back with your food, sir"*. As Jacob walks towards the door, he turns and looks at the patient. The tall man gives Jacob a thumbs up as he turns to sit back in the cold corner. Jacob walks out and locks the door behind him.

CHAPTER 4

As he made his way down to the kitchen, Jacob thought of getting some more updated magazines and maybe a newspaper for the patient to read. He also decided to find a better gown for him. It's a damn shame how people are treated here Jacob thought to himself. He knew that the staff would not approve of their loved ones living in these horrid conditions, and it angered Jacob that some staff didn't have any kind of compassion or respect for these people. It's bad enough that they were mentally insane, but to be constantly reminded that no one gives a shit about them nor their mental welfare was sad. Disappointment and internal anger began to rise in Jacob. He felt compelled to do something about the conditions of the patients. But what he could do? After all, he was a cheaply paid, young and dumb orderly, as Myrtice liked to point out.

He truly hated her. He even considered at one time going to school to become a nurse, just so he could take her job. She was just like the rest of the idiots who only were looking for a paycheck. Jacob came into the view of Groovy, the spunky cook for the hospital, dancing to the beat of Paul Simon's 'Call Me Al' from her radio. The medium- build brunette was one of the few staff members left that really cared for and was deeply concerned about the patients. *"Dinner order for the patient in room 477"*, Jacob announced as he gave her his ticket. She turned the paper over, looked over the list, and raised her eyebrows in shock. *"Oh wow, he's never written anything to me ever, Jacob"* Miss Groovy stated with a smile. *"I was shocked myself"*, said Jacob, *"But I'm happy that he's finally making some decisions and getting control over his dinner"*. *"Now Jacob, you know what the rules are- we can't deviate from the menu, but this time, I will. I don't know why the*

administrators and medical staff won't allow us to do
special orders for the patients. After all, this is home
for many of them. They won't be able to function well
outside of this god-forsaken building. They at least
need to make an effort to bring the morale up for these
poor people, `` said Miss Groovy as she eagerly begin to
make dinner for the patient in room 477. *"At least you*
and I think alike when it comes to these patients. It
burns me up to see them mistreated- but hey, what can
I do? Nothing, `` *said* Jacob with a look of defeat. *"Don't*
you ever say that Jacob", said Miss Groovy with a stern
but kind voice. *"I've seen how you interact with these*
patients. You are gentle, kind, and compassionate- a
rarity amongst these walls. You know what's in your
heart, and if you care for these patients as much as I do,
then we need to do something about the conditions here.
But we need to be careful. I've already heard staff
members whispering to each other about how you and I

are being 'too friendly' to the patients." As she made that statement, Jacob caught a glimpse of the wide load in white walking towards their direction. "*Shush,*" whispered Jacob to Miss Groovy. "*The charge horse, I mean nurse, is walking towards us.*" Miss Groovy spins around and places the fakest smile on her face. "*Top of the afternoon, Ms. Myrtice!*" she says as she puts her hands in her pocket, making sure Myrtice didn't see the menu from the patient in room 477. "*Oh shut up Groovy! Must you always be so cheery and nice ? Your bright spirit makes me ill*", snapped Myrtice as she gives Jacob a dirty look. "*And what the hell you think you're doing, punk! You're supposed to be checking up on that maniac! Where the hell have you been?*" "*If you must know*", snapped Jacob, " *I did go check on the patient. He gave me his menu and I decided to walk it down here instead of giving it to Old Man Jenkins. Fooling around with him, the patient in 477 will never get fed!*". "*Don't you get sassy with me!*" yelled Myrtice. "*And don't you call me no damn punk either, Miss Tubby!*" Jacob yelled back as Myrtice's and Miss Groovy's mouths both dropped to the floor. "*You're definitely ain't my favorite person, Myrtice, but I still show the upmost respect for you and I damn demand that you return the favor, since I do most of your fucking dirty work around here!*" For what seemed like minutes, there was dead silence as Myrtice's face turned as red as the smeared lipstick on her barely‑ there lips. "*Just‑get‑to‑work......please*", said the dejected charge nurse as she turned around and stomped her fat rear end back to her office. "*You can pick up your jaw off the floor now,*" laughed Jacob at Miss Groovy. "*Good for you Jacob. I'm so glad you stood up to her*" said Groovy. "*But please be careful. Myrtice doesn't take too kind to people challenging her authority. There have been a few over the years that have stood up to her‑ only to lose their job and their livelihood. Myrtice has many connections not only here in Dover but all over the state of Delaware, and many people have had the hardest time trying to find a new job after leaving here. Don't end up on her dirty list*". "*Forget her*", said Jacob. " *I need this food for my patient. He's my top concern now.*" As Miss Groovy fixed the patient's food, Jacob ran out of the dining area, down the hall, and snuck into the laundry room. In the back, he found new gowns that have not even been opened yet. Shaking his head, he grabbed two new gowns, towels and washcloths, and some clean sheets for the patient. On his way out, he saw today's newspaper, as well as some ESPN and Sports Illustrated magazines that didn't come out in the last century. He grabbed those, stuffed his stash in a plastic bag, and ran back into the kitchen. Miss Groovy had the food prepared. As Jacob grabbed the tray, Groovy asked him what was in the plastic bag. "*Oh, just some things that the patient in room 477 should have had a long time ago.*" Jacob smiled, thanked Miss Groovy and fast-walked back to the patient's room, being careful to avoid having anyone seeing the bag under his arm. He stood in front of the room, placed the bag between his legs and pulled the keys out of his pocket. As he turned the lock, he looked around to see if anyone was watching him. Sensing that the coast was clear, he hurried in and shut the door. The tall patient, still sitting in the corner, looked up at Jacob. A brightness, a glow that had never been there before, began to illuminate his face as Jacob walked towards him. His seemingly permanent frown turned upside-down as Jacob gave him his food tray and began to pull out the stash of goodies out the bag. "*I got ya' some updated magazines and today's newspaper. Imma try to sneak a newspaper in here every day that I'm working, okay?*" The patient nodded his head as he inhaled the four grilled turkey and cheese sandwiches and the tomato soup Miss Groovy so graciously made for him. Jacob put on gloves and put new sheets on the ragged mattress. He placed the mattress on the bed-frame, realizing that he forgot to grab a clean blanket. Jacob made a mental note to get that for the patient on his next encounter in the laundry room. He hid the towels and washcloths under the bed. *"Damn shame I gotta hide this; they act like they don't want you to look nor smell good"*. As the patient gave another thumbs up, Jacob pulled out a travel bottle size of body wash he'd managed to steal from the custodian's cart on the way back to the patient's room. Jacob bent down and whispered, *"Don't let them catch you with this. I ain't even s'posed to let you have this body wash"*. He placed it in the patient's hand. *"Now you hide that real good. I gotta get out of here before Myrtice makes her way to kill me. I told that witch off"* laughed Jacob as he and the patient gave each other a fist bump. The smile was wide and bright on the reclusive patient in room 477. He waved at the orderly as Jacob walked out the room. He looked down at the body wash, looked over to his newly made bed, the new gowns he desperately needed, and the sports magazines he was now eager to read. He begins to pick up one of the magazines to read but suddenly, he notices two shadows underneath the door. He carefully placed his tray on the floor, picked up all of his new goodies, and tip-toed over to one of the padded squares he made a few months ago when he was attacked. He could still remember slapping his hand imprint into the face of the tubby charge nurse when she called him a nigger and spit in his face. He'd never forget that day or what they did to him. Were they coming to do it to him again? Did they catch on to the actions of the kind, naïve orderly? Did they make him tell them what he'd done? The patient wasn't for sure, but he wasn't taking any chances. He carefully folded and flattened the gowns, towels, and washcloths. He hid the magazines and newspapers between the towels. As he slid his new belongings into the small slit, he took at glance at the paring knife he still had in his possession. He hurriedly tied the small strings back together so that the staff wouldn't notice, laid on his clean bed, and watched the shadows under his door as the key began to turn the lock.

CHAPTER 5

Thomas pulled into the driveway of their brick, Mediterranean-styled home. He caught a glimpse of Manny in the back seat, with ice cream all over his mouth and shirt. *"Dang Manny, I just gave you a bath before we left, now I gotta clean you all over again, and mom's gonna be so mad at me. I can hear her fussing now"*. As they get out the car, a white, newer model Mercedes CL with dark tinted windows pulls up besides them. A bright smile comes across Manny's face as his tutor, Miss Jayla Barnes, climbs out her car. She drives a nice car to be a part-time tutor and nurse assistant, thought Thomas as he tried to make sense on how she can afford such a luxury vehicle. Jayla has been a part of the Jenkins' family for years. Her mother; Bonnie used to work at the state prison in neighboring Tumbler County for years. Bonnie married after Jayla graduated from high school and moved to Texas. Jayla never knew her father; she was raised by her mom and her aunt Latrice. She went to the local community college and received her certification to be a teacher's assistant. She spent most of her years being a substitute teacher, bouncing from one daycare to another as an assistant, before landing a job with Dr. Crumbly. Dr Crumbley is Manny's doctor. She comes over three days a week to provide extra tutoring for Manny since he was deemed unfit by his father to go to school with other children. Manny has a teacher that comes over to home school him five days a week, so why the hell did my father hire Jayla, Thomas pondered to himself. As Jayla walks with Manny towards the house, Della meets her halfway up the walk path with a look of confusion. "*I thought Robert called you and cancelled your session today, Jayla.* Said Della" "*He did? I never received a phone call nor a message*", Jayla exclaimed with a look of confusion herself. *"I don't know, maybe Robert forgot. I'm sorry Jayla to have you drive all the way over here for nothing"* said Della. *"It's okay Mrs. Della; since I'm here, I'll help Manny get cleaned up. This will give me a chance to start showing him personal hygiene. I don't want to overwhelm him."* "Well", said Della with an unsure voice, *"If it's okay with Robert. He can be so ornery at times."I'll talk to him, if you don't mind Mrs. Della"*, assured Jayla. *"I'm sure he won't mind despite the miscommunication."* She walks with Manny inside the house, as Della and Thomas give her and each other a look of disapproval. *"Mama, I swear something's not right with her. She up to"*. Della cuts him off. *"Thomas, go in the house, and not another word from you about this."* Della shakes her head and walks behind Jayla. Thomas stands in the walk path, not sure of what to think about what just happened. Maybe it was a misunderstanding; maybe she didn't get the message. If she didn't get the message, why she didn't show up to the house with her learning materials she always have with her. Man, Mama so damn naïve, blind, and stupid, Thomas thought to himself. Somebody else besides him needs to start having some form of common sense. He turns around, heads to the street, and takes a stroll around the neighborhood to cool his rising temperature.

CHAPTER 6

"Are you crazy, are you fucking crazy Jayla!" Robert was livid as he rushed towards Jayla, grabbed her by the arms, picked her up, and slammed her against the car. As they argue in an alleyway down from Freida's, Jayla knees Robert in the stomach in an effort to loosen his grip. *"Don't you ever put your fucking hands on me again!"*, yelled Jayla. *"Why the hell you showed up to my house after I called and canceled Manny's tutor session? You knew damn well I called! You did get the message! What are you trying to do? What were you thinking?"*, said Robert. *"Robert"*, said Jayla, *"You have not been bringing Manny down to Doctor Crumbly for his appointments like you're supposed to! She's trying to be very nice and understanding, but I'm afraid she's going to call Child Protective Services soon. Robert, I don't know what the*

hell's going on in your household, but you have to put Manny's needs above everyone else's, including your own!" Robert glared at the frightened Jayla. "*I don't need no damn doctor telling me about my goddamn son Jayla! I'm his father! I know what he needs, I know what he doesn't need. I-*". "*Have you been giving him his medication, Robert?*" Jayla asked, cutting off his sentence. "*Oh....my....God Robert! You haven't been giving him his medicine! Do you want CPS to take your son away from you and Della? Think of the damage you will be doing to Manny! And Thomas? He'll never forgive you. Your relationship with Thomas is already strained. Maybe if you stop focusing on his basketball career, trying to live your life through his....*" Jayla stated before Robert cut her off. Robert grabs Jayla by the collar of her pink, floral blouse and puts his finger in her face. "*Don't you ever in your life mention my relationship with Thomas! It ain't none of yo' damn* *business! You do your job, take the payments I'm giving you to make your documents look good, and keep your mouth shut! You don't give a damn about Manny's needs either, otherwise, you wouldn't be sleeping with me!"* Touché muthafucka", smirked Jayla. *"You wouldn't be fucking me if you cared for Manny's needs also. And your damn cow of a wife followed me the entire time I did a pop-up to your house while I was cleaning Manny* `"What the hell were you expecting? She was sitting next to me when I called and canceled your session"*, said Robert. *"I'm sorry, I just wanted to see you. I haven't seen you in over two weeks. You keep cancelling Manny's tutoring sessions. I..just...miss...you."* Jayla looks up at Robert with tearful eyes and begins to walk to her car. Robert walks behind her and gives her a hug. *"I miss you too baby, it's just that these recruiters are going to be coming to the house the next several months and I've been busy* *preparing, making renovations, trying to make the house looks good. I've been trying to talk to Thomas about how to deal with all of this attention, especially this being his last year in high school. Don't worry, our time is coming soon. I have a recruiter coming over this weekend so we won't be able to see each other. But I promise baby I'll make it all up to you."* Jayla turns around to face Robert. They engage in a hug and a long, deep kiss. As they both let go, they exchanged goodbyes, get into their separate cars, and drive off. Unbeknownst to them, their actions were in full plain view of Freida Kristoff, who stood with her hands on her hips, her black, red, and green apron covering her medium, five feet frame. As she mumbled to herself in her thick, Jamaican voice, she was reminded of the kind, loving family that helped her and her family settle into Dover years ago from Kingston. The family who encouraged and supported her as she opened her own restaurant despite violence from the local KKK, as well as opposition from other blacks who were struggling with their flailing businesses. Freida vigorously shook her head, full of gray dreadlocks and walked back into her restaurant. With a heavy heart and the sudden flow of tears streaming from her big, brown eyes, she went into her office, closed her door, sat in her recliner chair, and contemplated her next move.

CHAPTER 7

Thomas yawned as he parked his car in the lot of Peak Ridge. As the crack of dawn began to light up the vast horizon, he sat and thought about all of the events that transpired in the past few days, as well as the beginning of his Senior year in school. What's really going on with his dad and Manny's tutor? Are they seeing each other? Why doesn't his mother confront his dad about Jayla and Manny's frequently missed tutor and doctor appointment? What is going on with her? Mama has changed so much over the years, thought Thomas as he pulled his University of Tennessee hoodie over his unkempt hair. *"Dang, I forgot to make an appointment with Chief to get my hair cut for school. I'll call him later"* said Thomas to himself as he got out of his car. With his headphones on, he programs his running music to old school rap. Thomas had an affinity for hip hop- real hip hop, not that mumble and drug-laden shit heard in unfortunate heavy rotation today. He locks his car, starts his playlist, puts his phone in his pocket, and begins his routine- stretching and running alongside the twists and turns of Peak Mountain. As he stretches, he becomes thankful for the only thing that he appreciated his father for. Robert ran this same trail in his younger years, and would always take Thomas with him. Thomas really enjoyed the past times he spent with his father- before Manny came into the world. After they would take their hour and a thirty-minute run, they would go to the picnic area near Peak Ridge and eat lunch, enjoy nature, and talk about life. The memories of his youth began to tug on Thomas' emotions, and his hardened heart towards his father began to fade away to regret. Thomas felt that maybe he was being too hard on his father. Thomas probably would have been upset and bitter if he'd torn his ACL during the fourth season in the NBA. That injury devastated Robert emotionally more than physically. Although he had saved up enough money for him and his family to live comfortably, Thomas knew that his father felt like he had failed him, his mom, Manny, and the community of Dover. As Thomas slowly started jogging out of the parking lot onto the path, he remembered all of the 'friends' who left his father's side when the money and fame ran out. No one gave his father any kind of emotional support, never paid a visit to the house, and stopped speaking to his father and the rest of the family. No calls from the high school to come and give motivational speeches to the children. The Booster Club basically abandoned him and took him off of the committee. In essence, no one gave a damn; all the pigeons took flight once the bread crumbs ran out. The talk of Robert being a failure, an embarrassment to the community, took a toll on Robert. He began to drink heavily; stayed out all night doing God-knows-what. Della would sleep in the basement after she grew tired of her husband's antics. She even temporarily left Robert and moved her and her boys into an apartment above Freida's restaurant. Thomas rounded the concrete path around the three-quarter mark on Peak Mountain, looking down at the rocky terrain that opened up to a beautiful view of the Lenape River. The sun began to peak out of the canvas of darkness, bringing a dull but beautiful shine to the calm waters. As he kept running, Thomas recalled the day that Manny was diagnosed with autism. His mom was devastated at first but she was thankful that he was finally given an official medical condition. The doctors could not figure out why Manny wouldn't speak, why he wailed for no apparent reason; and why he would spend hours and hours sitting by the pond in the back of the yard. The diagnosis would bring his parents back together, but the tension between them grew, as Robert and Della would constantly disagree over the manner in which Manny needed to be treated. Robert didn't believe in medications, and he strongly opposed Della sending Manny to a regular school. The children were cruel to Manny, and many teachers became impatient in dealing with him, whether it was due to a lack of knowledge about autism or just plain laziness. Della insisted that despite Manny's shortcomings, he still needed to receive an education and that his life needs to be as normal as possible. She agreed to the medications to a certain extent so that Manny would be able to function at an optimal level in order to be properly educated. Much to the dismay of Della, Thomas, and Dr. Crumbly, Robert decided to have Manny be taught at home and to have an extra tutor on certain days. Mrs. Mellencump is the home school teacher that comes and, of course, there is Jayla- who also assists with Manny's education at the insistence of Robert. Della could never figure out why Jayla was hired by Robert. Thomas has always had his suspicions about Jayla, but he knew his mother wouldn't hear of it. Thomas slows his pace as he goes uphill on the path. He puts more effort into his run as his thighs and hamstrings began to burn from the intensity the sharp hill brought. He loved all of the hard work he had put into his favorite sport, especially after getting a chance to work out with the University of Tennessee and Atlanta Hawks basketball camps this summer. He was greatly anticipating the return of school, not only to finish his senior year strong but to get a break from his family, including Manny. As much as Thomas loved Manny, having an autistic brother became exhausting, frustrating, and confusing. In his earlier years, Thomas' patient with Manny was very thin. He would become easily angered with Manny's frequent tantrums. But as he got older, and his parents became more argumentative, Thomas began to realize that he had to be patient with his brother. He knew he had to step up and be the drive that Manny needed to be as normal as possible. This growth is what sparked an interest in autism and mental health in Big T. Thomas' change of heart is the driving reason behind him wanting to concentrate more on his academics and education. The thought process of autistic children, along with the behavior of athletes interested him during his summer camp workouts. Thomas runs down the hilly path, passing the two-and one-half mile marker. He was extremely thankful for the crisp, August wind hitting his face, which was a welcome from the tumultuous heat waves that have blasted Dover all summer. The seasons were changing, and Thomas was looking forward to autumn, excited to see all of his friends, especially Jasmin. He and Jasmin have been friends for a long time. They always talked and encouraged each other in and out of school. Jasmin was a science junkie, always doing experiments, albeit dangerous at times. She even almost got expelled from school for blowing up the chemistry lab! Despite her troubles, she inspired to become a research scientist to find a cure for diseases like Sickle Cell Anemia and Alzheimer's Disease. Jasmin suffered from Sickle Cell disease, and was hospitalized a lot for crisis attacks. Despite her health, Jasmin never let her illness hinder her from doing what she was passionate about which was health and the effects on the black community. She received a full scholarship to the University of North Carolina, Chapel Hill to pursue a degree in Biomedical Sciences. Nearing the end of his run, Thomas runs off the path and cautiously enters the road, jogging towards the parking lot of Peak Ridge. As he goes into deep thought about his and Jasmin's futures, Thomas fails to notice the black, top-faded 1998 Ford Crown Victoria behind him. The car spots the tall figure in the bright orange hoodie running on the opposite side of the road. As the driver slows down, a smile of mischievous intentions slowly creeps on his cleanly shaven, caramel skin. He looks over to his passenger, who returns his approval of the driver's evil plan with a slow nod. The driver shifts his body closer to the steering wheel, getting a good look at his unsuspecting target. He pumps the brakes, slowly turning the car in the direction of Thomas. He places his foot on the gas pedal lightly, creeping upon Thomas, waiting for him to get closer to the yellow, wooden rail that separated the road from the steep, rocky terrain below. As Thomas nears the parking lot, he takes off his headphones and slows his pace. Lifting his phone up to catch a glimpse of the time, his phone suddenly lights up. The driver of the Crown Victoria has put on his bright lights. The passenger yells out, *"Fuck that nigga up my nigga!"* as the driver slams the gas pedal to the floor. Thomas spins around to see a car pummeling towards him! He drops his phone and the Beats and dashes towards his car. With his heart racing as if it was about to burst out of his chest, Thomas felt immense pain from his hamstrings. Sweat poured from his face as he gets the feeling in the pit of his stomach that his life was about to be over in a matter of seconds. He has to make a split decision! Thomas muttered to himself as mind raced for some resolution to his current situation. *"Should I run to my car? Who is this idiot behind the wheel? Why is he trying to kill me? Maybe I can run fast enough and jump over my car to lose him! What if I don't make it to my car"?* As he is running for his life, Thomas turns and sees that the car is inches away from him. Without giving it a second thought, Thomas turns, grabs the wooden guard rail, and jumps over, making a loud thud on the rocks before pummeling out of control towards the bank of Lenape River. With every hit and thump on the rocks, Thomas screams and cries for help, certain that he will be knocking on Heaven's door real soon. He is halfway towards his watery destination, maybe his grave, when his back suddenly hits a huge rock, stopping him from going any further. Bloody, bruised, and visibly shaken, Thomas makes a split decision to hide behind the rock, in case the driver of the car decided to get out to look for him. As much pain that he was in, Thomas managed to scurry behind the huge rock. He lies still for what seemed an eternity, holding his breath, being careful to not make any sound. He hears the car door slam-twice? What! There's someone else in the car with the maniac driver? Who's trying to kill me, thought Thomas as he began to pray- pray, like he's never prayed before in his life. Thomas doesn't even remember the last time he prayed to God for anything, but he knew that he needed Him at this very moment! His life flashed before his eyes, listening to the men talk about him. "*Did that punk roll into the river?*", snarled the passenger as he and the driver leaned over the guardrail. "*I hope so, but I'm not sure*", said the driver. "*I didn't hear a splash, but then again the only thing I heard was the roar of my engine*". The two fools laugh and high five each other. "*Should we go down and find that fake ass nigga?*", asked the driver, putting one leg over the rail. "*Hell yeah, let's go!*", said the tattooed passenger with dirty gold teeth and a blue skull cap covering his bald head. But as they began to climb over the rail, they heard the sound of a car coming in their direction. As the state trooper came around the bend, the car slowed down as it approached the two would-be murderers. They quickly changed their plan to hunt down Thomas as they walked back towards the car and waited. The state trooper stopped in front of the young men, rolled down her window, and glanced at them and the Crown Victoria pulled over to the side. *"Need some help, boys?"* she asked as she proceeded to open her door. *"No ma'am", said the driver. "We were just pulling over to check out the beautiful sunrise. I was about to take a picture, but my phone went dead'.* " *Damn them cell phones, huh,*" chuckled the passenger. The officer chuckled back. *"Yeah, technology can be a pain in the ass. Next time, carry you an old fashion Kodak instant camera. At least you don't need battery power for that'. You have a good morning officer",* said the driver. *"You two boys do the same,*" said the female officer. As they got into the car and pulled off, she waved, got back into her car, and drove away, all while making note of the suspicious car's license plate and description.

CHAPTER 8

As Thomas laid in agonizing pain behind the rocks, still trying to keep himself from being seen, he listened to the voices above his head talking to the police officer. Was that the same people that just tried to run over me? Or are these different people? What the hell was that about? Thomas wondered who the hell he's pissed off so bad to the point that they wanted to kill him. Thomas was known to be a bully in his younger days but all of that trouble was behind him once he managed to serve a small stint in juvenile detention for bringing a knife to school and threatening a classmate for making fun of Manny. Being in juvie for ninety days, Thomas had to mature quickly. He had missed his family, friends, and especially Manny. Thomas knew at that moment he had to change- change his attitude, change his thinking, change the people he hung around. After he completed his sting in juvenile detention, he started delving back into basketball, distanced himself from all of his bad-influencing friends (with the exception of Bumble), and started spending more time with Manny and learning about his disability. Thomas was extremely proud of himself for turning his life around. He did not want to disappoint his parents nor Manny ever in his life again. His grind to become the next NBA player out of Dover was on full throttle. He trained daily, all while education himself about Manny and his medications. He was not going to allow anyone or anything to deter him from achieving his lifelong goals. Thomas slowly turned to lie on his stomach. The pain was unbearable, but he knew he needed to grab onto the rock to get himself up. He cautiously peaked around the rock, not to alert anyone above that he was down on the rocky terrain. As he heard the cars drive away, he put one hand on top of the rock and the other hand on the left side. Thomas slowly dragged his left leg so that the top part of his foot was firmly placed in the ground. As he pushed with his left foot, he used the rock to pull himself up into standing position. He quickly became dizzy, and ended up bending at the waist, grasping the rock with his swollen, bloody hands. He lifted his head up to catch his equilibrium, and slowly came into a standing position. He turned around to look at the river, with its waters rolling by smoothly in a world filled with rough paths and chaos. The realization of near death enveloped his spirit, and he began to cry. Salty tears rolled down his face and as they caught the lacerations on his cheeks, they burned his face with such intensity Thomas vigorously rubbed his face, only making the matter worse. He trudged uphill towards the wooden rail and climbed over. As he walked towards his car, he realized that he dropped his phone and headphones somewhere during his sudden flight from the idiots that tried to run over him. He turned around and walked a few yards down the road to locate his belongings. *"Dammit! Where did I drop my phone?"*, yelled Big T loudly as he walked back to the area where he jumped over the rail. He didn't see his stuff in site. Man! What am I gonna tell dad now- I just had to get my phone replaced a couple of months ago. He will be pissed when I tell him I lost my phone again, thought Thomas as he finally got into his car. He grabbed his towel, wet it with the water from his bottle, and cleaned his battered face. As he looked up, he noticed what looked like a prison beyond the horizon, on the other side of the Lenape River. Hmmm, thought Thomas. He'd never noticed that building there before, after all these years of running the Peak Ridge trail with his father. Then again, they never parked in the parking lot either. They would always park around the bend, on the side of the road at the beginning of the trail. Thomas' curiosity

peaked as he stared at the grey prison. His instinct to

drive by there faded as he realized that he didn't have a

phone. Tired and fearful of the impending lecture he

was about to get from his father, Big T cranked the car,

pulled out the parking lot, and drove away, finally

thanking God for saving his life.

CHAPTER 9

Unbeknownst to Thomas, State Trooper Sylvia McArthur had picked up his cell phone and headphones that he had dropped. After the two hoodlums drove off, her detective intuition came into play. She had a gut feeling they were not at Peak Ridge to view the sunset. The car had matched a description that was given in a report a couple of weeks prior, in which another teenager had reported that the same car had attempted to run him over as he was walking home from his grandmother's house. As she was talking to the two troublemakers, she took note of the baby blue 1965 Chevy Impala that was parked in the lot. She assumed that the occupant of the car was running. She had performed a scan of the area when she noticed the cell phone and headphones on the ground. Thinking that it belonged to one of the two occupants of the Crown

Victoria, she headed back to the station to run a check on the phone. It was discovered that the phone had belonged to Thomas Jenkins of 1143 Brooke Light Street, in the affluent neighborhood of Brooke Caven. As she pulled into the driveway of the Jenkins home to return his belongings, she takes note of the baby blue Chevy Impala coming up behind her- the same car she saw in the parking lot at Peak Ridge. Thomas also spotted the state trooper, and once again his heart began to pound. Was this the same officer he heard talking above his head as he lay on the ground? Is she here to ask about me? Thomas got out of his car and walked up in front of the officer- he didn't want her to get anywhere near the front door. *"May I help you, ma'am?"*, said a nervous Thomas, as he tried to not give her much eye contact. *"Are you Thomas Jenkins?"*, asked State Trooper McArthur, sensing his nervousness. Thomas nodded. *"I found your cell phone* and headphones up by Peak Ridge. *They must have fallen out of your pocket*". "*Yes ma'am*", said Thomas. "*I run up there on the trail, and I didn't realize that my stuff was missing, until- until I finished my run*". Thomas had almost blurted out the real reason for dropping his phone and headphones, and his hesitation did not go unnoticed by the officer. "*Tell me, Thomas. Did you see a black, older model Crown Victoria with a faded rooftop up there?*", asked Trooper McArthur, attempting to get Thomas to talk. "*No, can't say that I did officer*", said Big T. "*How did you get those lacerations on your face, Thomas*", asked the officer with curiosity. "*I ran into a few hanging branches on the trail as I was running, officer. It was pretty dark when I was running, and the lighting on the trail isn't too good*", Thomas lied as the officer raised her eyebrow at his peculiar answer. "*Well, next time be careful, and be mindful of things falling out of your pocket. People still* have sticky fingers, and this phone could have gotten into the wrong hands", said Sylvia McArthur as she reaches into her car to get his belongings. Thomas begins to remove his hands out of his pockets to retrieve his belongings but realizes that his hands are still swollen with traces of dried blood still present. "Officer, do you mind putting my stuff on top of my car? It's freezing out here, and I don't want to take my hands out of my pockets." "Certainly Thomas", said the officer and she placed his phone and headphones onto the driver's seat of his car. "Thank you so much officer. Now, let me move my car- I have you blocked in". As the officer turns towards her car door, Thomas quickly jumps behind the wheel and proceeds to park in front of his house. Trooper McArthur backs out and pulls alongside him. "You're welcome Thomas, and if there's anything you need to tell me or just need my help, please let me know. You can call the North Station located in Mulsville and *ask for State Trooper McArthur. I would give you a card but they haven't made any for me yet. I'm still new to this career*. "*I will be sure to reach out to you if I need anything*", smiled Thomas, despite intense pain to his face. The state trooper drives off, taking note of Thomas backing into his driveway. She was determined more than ever to get to the bottom of that bullshit story Thomas fed her, especially after noticing Thomas' swollen and bloodied hands when he initially got out the car. She wasn't sure what was going on, but she was sure about one thing- the black Crown Vic and the young men in the car were somehow tied to Thomas and the other teenager who reported almost being ran over weeks ago. Watching the state trooper drive off, Thomas surmised that she didn't believe the lie she told him. But he didn't want to think about it. He didn't want her to know the truth at that moment. In fact, Thomas desperately needed to get into the house and take a shower without his parents noticing his superficial injuries. He really needed to talk to Bumble now- the black, faded top Crown Victoria jogged his memory. Those fools, whomever they were, used the same car to try to kill Bumble a couple of weeks ago when he was walking home from his grandmother's house!

CHAPTER 10

Thomas blows the whistle. *"Alright y'all boys, back to the line. We need to run these drills again. And we gon' keep doing them 'til ya'll get 'em right. No complaining!"* The young teens and preteens at the Save Our Children Youth Center grumbled as they trudged back to the end of the basketball court. The youth basketball league were training for their preseason exhibition game, and Thomas was selected as one of the assistant coaches. Thomas was grateful to Jasmin for introducing him to Mr. Ray Hudson, the president of the youth center. Mr Ray allowed him to complete his volunteer hours. This opportunity was also a much needed outlet from the recent events that have haunted him. Not only was he still in pain from his tumble at Peak Ridge, he was even more paranoid than before. The pain and mental anguish was inhibiting him from his own basketball training. He was trying to avoid taking any pain medication, and even worse, he still hadn't told his parents yet about the horrifying incident. Bumble and him had not spoken since the incident at Freida's Ice Cream Parlor. He really needed to catch up to Bumble to see if he knew anything about the hoodlums that tried to kill him. As the kids started their drills, Thomas noticed Jasmin talking to some tall, lanky kid with a low fade haircut and short dreadlocks on the top. Who the hell is that, thought Thomas. Thomas has always had feelings for Jasmin, but he kept them to himself. He was assured that Jasmin would never feel the same way for him. She would tell Big T how he was always the brother she wish she had. They were close friends and he knew she wanted to keep it that way so he was never tempted to cross the line. An ounce of jealousy came over Thomas as he walked towards Jasmin and her male friend. *"Hey Big T, so I've* heard you're getting these kids in line for their upcoming game! And Mr. Hudson has nothing but praise and adoration for the way you interact and talk to them about sports and life", said Jasmin, giving Big T a tight hug. Thomas' heart fluttered, but he kept his feelings at bay. "Yeah, I'm just grateful to be here, and Manny is over in the learning center with his home school teacher having a good time. It's good to be back in my element" said Thomas, shooting a look of curiosity at the kid next to Jasmin. "Pardon my manners Thomas. Thomas, this is a former volunteer and participant here at the youth center, Jacob Collins. Jacob, this is my good friend Thomas Jenkins" Jasmin said as she introduced them. The young men nodded their heads in silent acknowledgement. "So, you still leaning towards the University of Tennessee?", asked Jacob. "For the time being, yeah, but you never know what the future holds. I may change my mind", said

Thomas. *"Must be nice, having connections and all'* Jacob stated with sarcasm. *"And exactly what the hell you mean by that? Nigga, you don't even know me. I put 100 in every damn thing I do!"*, replied Thomas with a look of disgust, hands slowly forming into a fist. The gym quieted down as the kids and other adults turned their attention to the minor verbal altercation. *"Just what the hell I meant, Niggaaaa"*, snapped Jacob, returning the look of disgust. *"Look Jasmin, thanks for the advice on the nursing program. I'll look into it. And if you need to do any observation for your medical program at school, let me know. I can get you on with one of the doctors."* They gave each other a hug and Jacob walked off, eyeing Thomas with abhorrence. *"Who the hell is that lame?"*, said Thomas as he watched Jacob walk off. *"Oh, Jacob?"*, said Jasmin. *"He's a good kid. Not sure why he said what he said to you. He graduated from high school last year and is working as*

Mind Under Troubled Waters | 67

an orderly or nurse's aide, whatever they call it. He was asking about getting into nursing school at the local community college. And he's trying to start his dog breeding business. A really good kid." "Well, he lucky these kids are here. He almost got dealt with", muttered Thomas, careful not to let the kids hear him. *"Big T, you have to control your temper. These kids really look up to you and they emulate everything you do. You have to be positive and remain calm in every situation. And besides, Mr. Hudson will get rid of you if you keep doing these outbursts. Man, what's wrong with you? Lately, you've been acting real strange, very distant. Is everything okay? And what's wrong with your face? Look like you landed face-first in a pile of thorns."* Thomas wanted to tell her the recent events at Peak Ridge and his suspicions of his father and Jayla. *"Dang Jasmin, I'm good. I know how to behave. Stop talking to me like you my mama!"* "I'll talk to you *however I want to, Thomas. You need to get yourself together and get your ego off your shoulders. Ego will be your career killer.*", Jasmin shot back and walked off, with tears forming in her eyes. What the hell is wrong with Big T. He's never talked to me like that, thought Jasmin, as she stormed out of the gym. She was so upset about the encounter she failed to notice the four guys that brushed past her and walked inside. Thomas sat on the bench while the kids continued their drills, head buried in his hands. He felt ill for talking to Jasmin like that. Dang, I need to get it together and put my temper in check, thought Thomas. The pressures of life were beginning to wear on him. As his mind started to drift, the voices of kids interrupted his dark thoughts. *"Hey man, get off the freaking court! We trying to have practice! Coach Thomas, please get these fools off the court!"* Thomas jumped off the bench to see four knuckleheads, presumably the same age as him, running the court with the balls they took from the kids. *"Hey, get off the court! If you want to play ball, use the courts outside, and not in here"*, yelled Thomas as he ran towards one that had a black leather and suede jacket with the initials JRHS on the left sleeve. The heckler turned to Thomas and threw the ball, hitting Thomas in his face. All hell broke loose as Thomas quickly recovered and ran after the punk. The three other boys that came in with the leathered jacket fool sprinted outside also. Lingering pain from the Peak Ridge incident struck Thomas as he chased down and finally caught up with the guy. Thomas pummeled the kid's face with his slightly swollen hands. *"Man I will fucking kill you if you ever throw that damn ball in my face again!"* *"Man get yo' ass offa me!"*, yelled the pinned down kid as he attempted to avoid the thunderous blows Thomas was delivering. The other three guys arrived and attempted to jump on Thomas, but the other male adults that worked at the youth center managed to pull them away. Mr. Hudson and another man pulled Thomas off and pinned him down to the concrete sidewalk. *"Get the hell out of here you juvenile rugrats, and if I catch you here again, I'll have all of you arrested!"*, Mr. Hudson screamed at the four intruders. The leathered jacket hoodlum glared at Thomas. *"This ain't ova nigga! Your day coming! The next time I see you, Imma kill you on the spot!"* They ran towards the parking lot, jumped into a white Ford F150, and peeled out. As Mr. Hudson assisted Thomas to his feet, Thomas turned and looked at the disappointing looks on the faces of the kids. *"I'm so sorry"*, lamented Thomas, choking back tears. *"It's okay"*, said one of the kids. *"We like you a lot Coach Thomas. Thanks for helping us get ready for our game and for running those bullies off the court. They used to do that to us all the time at the court by Jackson Rolle*

High School. That's why we don't play over there anymore". The kids all ran up to Thomas and gave him a hug. After they ran back inside the gym, Mr. Hudson came up and looked at Thomas in the face. "*Thanks young blood; I really appreciate you being here and having a great influence on the kids. Jasmin spoke highly of you and I'm glad I made the right choice in allowing you to volunteer and mentor these kids. They really love and appreciate you*" stated Mr Hudson. "*I don't know if I'm a great influence on these kids now. I totally lost my temper, and they witnessed it*", said Thomas with disappointment. "*Don't worry about it*", said Mr. Hudson. "*I know you had to defend yourself. I'd beat the brakes off anyone who intentionally hit me in the face with a basketball.*" They both laughed and headed back into the gym. Thomas took a mental note of the letters on the jacket and the words the kid told him about Jackson Rolle. He picked up his keys, walked to his car, and tried to call Bumble, but no answer. Jackson Rolle High School, Thomas thought to himself. That's all the way over in Melfair County, damn near two hours away from Dover. Why in the hell would these guys come all the way over here to act like idiots. Did these guys have something to do with him getting nearly smashed at Peak Ridge. Suddenly, the adrenaline wore off, and the agonizing pain came in with intense rage. "*Dang*", said Big T. "*This pain just don't seem to wanna go away. I can't take much more of this, but I don't want anyone to know about my near death experience.*" Thomas grabbed his phone, called his barber, and set up an appointment to get a haircut along with six 'Blue Diamonds'.

CHAPTER 11

The melodious sounds of the bombastic band could be heard miles away. Orientation was the highlight of the beginning of another school year for the students, faculty, and other staff at James S. Middleton High School. As the Jenkins family, minus Manny, desperately tried to find a parking space closer to the auditorium, they realized all hope was lost in getting Della closer to the ramp. She has a cyst in both knees, and the struggle to walk to the bathroom daily let alone a long path to the auditorium was a daunting task. They ended up parking all the way in the back on the grass by the agriculture building. *"I'll stay in the car",* said *Della. "My pain just won't allow me to trek up that ramp".* *"Okay- let's go T",* said Robert, leaving the keys inside the ignition. Good, Thomas said to himself. He definitely didn't want his mother to come inside, and he needed to lose his father so that he could find Bumble to tell him about his mishap on Peak Ridge and at the youth center. They had been asking incessantly about his swollen hands and the lacerations on his face. Also, Thomas had been experience pain and spasms resulting from him hitting that rock at Peak Ridge. He had been trying to walk as normal as possible, as to not draw any more attention to himself. He didn't want his parents to know the real truth, he didn't want to see the doctor, and he didn't want anyone to know that he was back on prescription drugs to help his mind again. As father and son walked towards the auditorium, Robert placed his hand on Thomas' left shoulder. Thomas, still in pain from his tumble, managed to control his reaction to the pressure that was on his shoulder. *"Thomas, I just want you to know that I'm so proud of you. I also want to say that I'm sorry for pressuring you over the years. I just want what's best for you, and being stuck here in dead-*

end Dover is not the kind of future I envision for my son. If you need anything, and I mean anything, I'm here for you. I love you Big T and I always will' Thomas nearly came to tears. It's been a long time since his father told him he loved him. He's hasn't seen this sincerity from Robert since he was a young boy, taking their runs on Peak Ridge. *"Thanks Dad. This means a lot to me. I love you too, and I'm proud of the man that you have been to me, mom, and Manny, despite a few rough patches. I do want to talk to you about something that I've been interested in doing, but we can save that conversation for another time. Let's just go inside and get this boring shit over and done!"* Robert cocked his head towards Thomas, laughing loudly. *"Don't think you too grown to get yo' ass knocked out boy! Better watch your damn language. "* They both laughed and headed inside the auditorium.

After hearing the same, boring, speeches from the principal, assistance principals, and other administrators, Robert and Thomas look over Thomas' schedule for the year. Thomas had selected his electives after talking with Jasmin at Frieda's, and he noticed his dad's look of surprise and confusion. *"Medical terminology? Early childhood education? Social Issues and Mental Health in Society? What kind of electives are these? What's your aim, Thomas?"* asked Robert.

"*Dad*", said Thomas. *"That's what I had wanted to talk to you about later but since we're on the subject- I've become more interested in Manny's disability and mental illness, especially in the black community. Don't get me wrong, Dad, basketball is my passion- but it isn't the only thing. I've been really wanting to get my grades up and excel not only on the court, but off the court too"*. Big T glanced at his father, only to notice that he was looking at the school's basketball Hall of

Fame and all of the records he set back in the 60's, not giving any thought nor response to Thomas' desires. "*Never mind*," Thomas said under his breath with disgust as they headed to Coach Baptiste's office to discuss the upcoming basketball season. They neared the glass-enclosed cafeteria and strolled past to get to the double doors that lead outside to the athletic department. Thomas looks over to his right and sees Bumble sitting inside the cafeteria talking to members of the football and basketball team. "*Dad, you go ahead of me, I'll catch up. I have to talk to Bumble- it's urgent*". "*Alright T, but don't be too long*", said Robert as he pushes the door open. Thomas runs into the cafeteria towards the crew, who suddenly become silent as he comes upon them. Obviously, they were talking about me, but about what, Thomas thought as they all dapped and saluted each other. "*Damn T, what the hell happened to yo' face?*", exclaimed Skully as the rest of the crew around Thomas stared. *"Man you won't believe this fuck shit we just heard!"*, exclaimed Bumble as the rest of the young boys spoke and nodded in agreement. Thomas looks in bewilderment as the wide receiver of the football team, Tayvon "Noble" Martin, eyes widened as he opened his mouth to speak. *"Man, tell me why the fuck Coach Baptiste done went and recruited some supposed top notch basketball player from Jackson Rolle High my nigga. Damn Big T, Baptiste buggin' as hell. I wonder what Mr. Qualm had to say about this? Is he a part of this plan also? I never expected Coach Baptiste to pull some slick shit like this! That's some straight fucked up mess!"* Thomas nearly fainted! Jackson Rolle High School? He recalled the letters on the jacket of the jerk that he beat the living hell out of. So these guys are from Jackson, and he was sure they came to the youth center to taunt and harass him, Thomas thought to himself with incensed anger. *"The fuck ya'll heard this weak shit from, and where this nigga at now?"*, said Thomas, feeling the rage of fire burning in his throat. *"Man, we heard this bull yesterday morning. Big T, did you get any of our calls and texts? We've been blowin' up yo' damn phone all day yesterday! The fucks goin'on wit' you man?"*, said Allan, one of the forwards for the basketball team. *"Man, y'all just don't know. I had a fucked up day yesterday. I didn't charge my phone before I left for the youth center, and the past couple of weeks have been rough as shit!"*, said Thomas, recalling the events of Peak Ridge and the basketball practice with nervousness. *"Why the hell would Baptiste even go trying to get other players,"* said Bumble. *"We got great players on our team now. Our flow is tight, and we don't need no damn strange ass niggas comin' in messing up nothin'. And besides, I also heard Baptiste trying to get three more players from Jackson Rolle to* come to our school. *What the hell's going on, Big T?*

They trying to replace us. Apparently, this top notch

nigga supposed to be playing the same position you

play. And the other three supposed to be playing the

same positions me, Allan, and Joker play." "*Aww, hell*

naw!", yelled Big T, getting the attention of the others in

the cafeteria, including a mysterious new student with

bright, dyed blonde dreadlocks, sitting in the corner, out

of sight of the angry group of athletes. *"Ain't no*

muthafucka comin' up in here taking my damn place! I

work too hard for this shit! Been bustin' my ass all

summer, all my life, and I ain't gon' let some bitch ass

nigga take my place, I don't give a fuck who it is!",

shouted Thomas, as he stormed off to Coach Baptiste's

office, with the other players behind him in full pursuit.

Slamming doors and cursing towards the athletic

department, the dreadlocked kid sitting in the corner

shook his head and smiled to himself. He got on the

phone, waiting for the person on the receiving end to answer. Going straight to voicemail, he left a message- *"Aye yo, just spotted that nigga Big Thomas and his dick-riders leaving the cafeteria going to Baptiste office. Yeah, this nigga a hothead, just like Baptiste said. Man, you ain't got shit to worry about. That spot on this weak ass team, that basketball scholarship to the University of Tennessee basketball team. It's all yours, homie. We just got to get Tennessee to take they minds offa Big T and focus on you."* As he hung up, the phone rung. *"Nigga, why you let me leave that damn voicemail? You shoulda picked up the phone when I called"*, said the mysterious new student. *"Man"*, said the new top recruiter from Jackson Rolle High. *"We gots us a damn problem! Went to the community center yesterday and saw that nigga Big T; almost jumped his ass for disrespectin' me but I kept it cool"*, lied the new recruiter. *"We found out this nigga daddy was a star*

NBA player for the Celtics back in the day, so you know he know some peeps that can get his son on. *And what's even worse, Punk T got some major pull in his godfather, who's a top basketball recruiter. The heat need to be turned up, my nigga, know-what-I'm-sayin'? Yo' drugged up ass cousins didn't get the job done out there at Peak Ridge! I want the nigga permanently injured, not killed! Tell yo' cousins to stay off them coke lines and get Big T where it hurts- that right leg he injured years ago". "Cool, man, cool". I'll talk to Lil' Reg and Bricks. These niggas can't keep fuckin up. They already fucked up once before trying to take out Big T's fake ass, suicidal friend Bumble".* "*Just tell them to keep the shit on the low, real cool*", said Takeout, the top notch from Rolle High. "*And don't tell anybody how much money Baptiste paid me, Augustin, Pierre, and Julien to come to this hell-hole to play*". "*Neva that*", said Dreadhead, the new student with the dyed blonde 'locks. He ended the call, exited the cafeteria, and hid in the storeroom next to Baptiste's office, hearing screaming and yelling coming from the angry athletes.

CHAPTER 12

"Ohhhh! Ohhhhh! Aaaaaaughh!" The cringing sounds of Manny screaming, coupled with the loud thuds heard from his head pounding against the leather ottoman, had Robert, Della, and Thomas rushing into the study room where Manny receives his home schooling. Manny was flapping his body, displaying one of his "unbearable tantrums"as Jayla described them. *"What the hell is wrong with him, Jayla?"*, shouted Robert, as Manny's wailing became louder and louder. *"Oh, he's just throwing one of his unbearable tantrums again. I was trying to show him how to sort and count money and he became upset"*, said an exasperated Jayla, standing in front of Manny with her hands on her hips. *"Maybe he's had enough for today. You've been going at this all day with him, Jayla. You can't force Manny to do something that he doesn't want"*, said

Della. "*He needs to learn to do something on his own, Della*", said Robert, throwing her a dirty look. Jayla felt the same way in regards to Manny's behavior. Della always have a dang excuse for everything, thought Jayla. The three adults attempted to calm Manny by grabbing him, but he was too powerful. Now he was throwing himself harder against the ottoman, and alternating between his hand flapping and covering his head with his favorite Spiderman blanket. Thomas just stood in the midst behind the three adults, looking at his brother with sadness. He knew exactly what was going on, and he did not appreciate Jayla speaking about his brother in the manner she was. The words she used were offensive, and his sadness quickly turned into rage. He walked up to Jayla, got straight in her face, and put his finger on her forehead. "*He's not having an 'unbearable tantrum', you uneducated dumbass. He's having a sensory autistic meltdown.*

You can't continue to overstimulate his mind and his sensory organs. Autistic children need a break as much as regular children, even ignorant, stupid adults as yourself! I don't know why the fuck my dad even hired you to begin with! You're a pathetic waste of a human being. This so-called tutoring you provide to my brother, I can do so much better without my parents having to pay you to come over and waste Manny's time and their money! Maybe these ten pounds of makeup, twenty pounds of perfume, and these tight ass clothes you wear every time you come over here got your mind warped, but don't you ever, in your fucked up, insignificant life, talk down about my brother ever in your life again"! Everyone in the room stopped and looked at Thomas; even Manny's wailing became a little more quieter. Jayla had a stunned look on her face as if she physically got slapped. Not known to them, Manny's home school teacher, Mrs. Mellencump, stood

Mind Under Troubled Waters | 87

in the entryway to the study room, with a smile on her face. Thomas had came to her a while back, eager to learn about autism. She had been working with Thomas, showing him things about Manny, even letting Thomas come to the autistic camps she runs at the youth center so he gain exposure to other children and adults with the disability. Robert recently found out about Thomas taking Manny down to the youth center . He didn't agree with any of this, never cared for Manny to go along with Thomas, and he wasn't too keen on Thomas having a sudden interest in autism and mental health. He really desired for Thomas to focus on basketball, but he kept his mouth shut for the time being; at least the break from Manny gave him the opportunity to spend more time with Jayla. Mrs. Mellencump walked over to Thomas and put her hands on his shoulders. *"Remember Thomas, there has to be a lot of patience learned and practiced by everyone who deal with individuals with autism*". She gave Jayla a menacing glare as Thomas backed away from her.

"*Jayla, Manny is not throwing a tantrum, and I would appreciate it if you would not ever mention that word again! When Manny has his sensory meltdowns, it is best if all of you would allow the meltdown to take its course, ensuring Manny's safety at all times!*", said Mrs. Mellencump. "*Out of everyone in this room, I would have expected a better handling of this situation from you. After all, Jayla, you do have your certification in childhood education with special training in children with autism, right?*", Mrs. Mellencump said with a tone of sarcasm. The scowl forming on Jayla's face would have killed everyone standing in the study room, if it could. Thomas formed an evil smirk on his face as his brown eyes deadened on Jayla's overly made-up face. Attention was now focused on Manny, who was more calm than before but still inconsolable. Thomas walked into his room, and retrieved his headphones and his iPad. He came back into the room and gently scooped Manny into his hands. As they sat in the ottoman, Manny calmly whispered to Manny, "*It will be okay. Here, listen to some music*". He placed the headphones on Manny's head, and proceeded to play classical music. Manny's tense body became more relaxed, and he slowly began to rock back and forth in Thomas' lap, finally falling asleep. Thomas picked himself and his brother off the ottoman and carried Manny into his room and placed him in his racer car bed. He watched his brother sleep for a few minutes, thinking of his behavior towards Jayla. He suddenly began to feel guilty. He knew better than to approach Jayla in an aggressive manner, but he just didn't understand why Jayla has to be a part of Manny's education to begin with. She's very impatient with him, hardly pays any attention to Manny when she does come over, and is as dumb as a box of rocks, but none of that excused his behavior towards her. Thomas has worked so hard on controlling his rages since he finished his stint in juvenile detention. But lately, he's been having a hard time keeping his anger at bay. His relationship with his father has been more tense; he's at odds with the basketball coach over another transfer player possibly taking his position; the pain from his tumble at Peak Ridge has been going on for weeks were getting worse, the fight he got into with the kids from Jackson Rolle High deflated his ego. He'd been taking Flexeril his classmate stolen from his father to relieve spasms, as well as the 'Blue Diamonds' he was buying from his barber. He was in desperate need to see a doctor, but he was afraid that the doctor would tell him that he couldn't play basketball. Those were words that he did not want to hear, so self-medicating was his only choice. And hallucinations!· He's been experiencing more hallucinations.. Thomas knows deep down that he's sick, but his only focus is basketball, school, and Manny. Thomas gave his brother a kiss on the forehead, covered him, and quietly exited the room, leaving the door slightly ajar. The guilt of lashing out at Jayla was overbearing, so he sought out her to apologize. He went back to the study room to find her, but she wasn't there. Maybe she had already left, thought Thomas; he didn't blame her if she did. He ran down the stairs and into the dining room. His mom was sitting at the table with Manny's teacher, trying to settle her nerves. *"Mom, have you seen Jayla? I need to see her, I"*. *"Thomas, I think you have already done enough damage for the day"*, said Della. *"You have not been acting yourself lately. I haven't seen you so incensed like this in a long time. Are you okay? What's the matter with you? I know you love and care about your brother but this is not the way to behave!"* *"Mom, I'm sorry, but I really need to find Jayla and apologize*", said Thomas. "*I think she's gone already, but you can try to see if she's still outside*," said his mom. Thomas dashed out of the door, but unfortunately, Jayla's car was gone. Dammit!, thought Thomas. He'd missed her. Feeling defeated, Thomas decided to take a walk; he needed to clear his head. His mom was right; he hasn't been acting himself lately. He knew he had to get himself and his life back together. He felt as if his world was coming apart.

Thomas had walked to the end of his street - his intentions were to turn around and walk to the other end, but his instincts told him to make a left turn and walk towards the community park in their subdivision.

CHAPTER 13

As he walked, he replayed the events at the house earlier in his mind. The way he approached Jayla, the anger he felt when she spoke ill about Manny⁻ he just didn't understand why she used those words. He was confused as to why his parents didn't step in and defend him and Manny. Did they feel the same way about Manny that Jayla felt? Thomas felt as if he was alone in the world; like he and Mrs. Mellencump were the only one who actually cared about Manny. Suddenly, a familiar object⁻ two familiar objects⁻ came into his sight! He hurriedly ducked behind a car parked on the street. As he peeped his head from around the car, he could see the two familiar objects, but he couldn't see the owners of the cars he knew so well. He made a quick decision to approach the park from the entryway on the next street over.

Catching a glimpse of his surroundings, he dashed between the houses and onto the next street. He cautiously walked up to the main entrance of the park, taking note of anyone who might notice him. As he got into the park, he snuck behind a large oak tree. He stared, and stared, and stared at the offending sight ahead of him. About ten feet away from him, he viewed his father and Jayla holding and kissing each other! *"What the hell is this!"*, Thomas whispered to himself. He knew it! He had a feeling there was something else going on between Jayla and his dad. *"This whore been sleeping with my dad this entire time she's been 'tutoring' Manny. Tutoring my ass, she ain't worth a shit!"* All of Thomas' anger and disdain for Jayla was warranted. No way in hell was he gonna apologize to that home wrecking bitch now. And Robert? Why? How? How could he do this to his mom, to Manny, to all of them. Robert wasn't the best father to them nor the best husband to Della, but Thomas would have never thought in a million years that his dad would cheat on his mom. Thomas listened closely to their conversation, trying to keep his anger from boiling over. *"Robert, I need to go. I do not want anyone to ride by and see us. I told you we should have met at the grocery store down the road."* *"And I told you that I told Della I was going to see Mr. Barnes down the street. Della knows it doesn't take long for me to get to his house. She doesn't even know I drove in the car."*, said Robert. *"I'll say this"*, said Jayla. *"If your son ever gets in my face like that again, I'll slit his fucking throat! How dare he talks to me like that! And why didn't you nor your damn wife say anything to him. And that crackkka? His teacher? She got some fuckin' nerve speaking to me like that! Why didn't you step in and defend me, Robert?"* *"Because you were dead ass wrong, Jayla!"*, yelled Robert. *"Hell, I wanted to slap the shit out of you myself! You don't talk to my son like that. Thomas was*

right! You really don't know what the hell you're doing

when it comes to Manny! Why am I paying you to tutor

Manny?" Jayla glared at Robert, on the verge of tears.

"Are you serious right now? You asshole, you're paying

me to make this paperwork look good so that you can

continue to get paid to buy the medications that you

haven't been giving to Manny! You just taking

advantage of the system, just like me! You are no better

than me, with your trifling ass! I'm only doing a favor

for you so Dr. Crumbley won't report you to Child

Protective Services for withholding your son's

medications. So, what praying miracle oil, water, or dirt

has Rev. Jackson come up with now? You praying and

paying him, and neither him nor God has answered

your prayers! You ". Before Jayla could finish her

sentence, her face was met with the palm of Robert's

large hand. He slapped her so hard she fell back and

tumbled off the bench. *"Fuck you bitch! You better not ever talk about God, Rev. Jackson, my wife, nor my kids ever in your pathetic life again. You ain't nothin' but a cheap, worthless ass hoe! I should have kicked your ass to the curb a long time ago after I found out you were sucking the life and dick out of Rev. Jackson's son! That's a way to get down and pray on your knees-literally! Looks like you were trying to seek God yourself- through worldly ways!"* Thomas damn near passed out upon seeing and hearing the latest foolishness. He couldn't believe what he was hearing! And slapping Jayla the way he did! That was totally uncalled for, even for Robert. His father always taught him to never put his hands on a woman. Thomas had never witnessed his father hitting Della ever in his life. Hell, Robert would walk away whenever he and Della got into heated arguments. Walk away son, just walk away- these were the words that Robert echoed to his son all the time. Never hit a woman ever! Not only was Robert an abuser, he was a walking contradiction. And what about this business with Robert not giving Manny his medications? What did Jayla have to do with any of this madness? Did his mom know? Did Mrs. Mellencrump have any knowledge of this? And what about Dr. Crumbley? Surely she has no idea. Dr Crumbley was very adamant about Manny getting proper treatment. She would have been reported Robert and Della to Child Protective Services- she's done it before when Manny started missing too much school. Thomas slumped behind the oak tree, overwhelmed by the shocking events of the day, as he continued to listen to his dysfunctional dad. *"Don't you ever come to my house again! Fuck you Jayla! I can take care of my own son. I don't need you. And Mrs. Mellencrump lucky the state is watching my ass like a hawk, otherwise, I'd fire her ass too! None of you are worth a shit, not even my own fucking wife! Hell, I don't know if I even care for my own children!"* "*You're crazy!*", yelled Jayla, picking herself up and charging towards Robert. Robert grabbed the front of Jayla's face and shoved her back to the ground. *"Don't come near me again! It's over, Jayla. Don't come to my house, don't come near my family again! I'll have your ass fucked over and put away for life! I've done it before, and I'll do it again!"* What!, Thomas thought to himself. What the hell his dad meant by that? He was too distraught to even think about it. He knew he had to get home, and tell his mom everything that he knew. He jumped up, almost tripping over the roots of the oak tree, sneaking quickly out of the park and sprinted home leaving Jayla lying on the grass.

CHAPTER 14

The patient in room 477 sat against the wall of his room with scorn as Myrtice, Big Rich, Sheldon, and Mr. Gunner stood over him. Palpitations hit his chest wall like a jackhammer against concrete. He wasn't sure what was about to go down; all he knew that whatever was about to happen, it wasn't going to be good- for anyone. He was determined to defend himself at all costs without the knife. He'd wished he would have kept the knife he'd pulled off of Sheldon during the last beatdown in his hand, but he put it back in the secret place in the padded wall. He'd wondered if they had forced Jacob to tell them about the things he'd gave to him. He almost wished Jacob would have minded his business. The patient in room 477 didn't want anything bad to happen to the orderly; he knew what these racist, brutal staff members were capable of doing. *"Get the* fuck up, you schizo, fucked- up- in- the- head-ass nigger!", yelled Myrtice. Her body odor was beyond offending, to the point where the patient in room 477 had to control his nausea. He refused to follow the overweight cow's demands. "Nigger, didn't she tell you to get up! That means get yo' black ass up now boy!", snapped Sheldon as he, Big Rich, and Mr. Gunner proceeded to snatch him to his feet. "Ain't finna be too many mo' of yo' niggers and boys much longer, you redneck crackas!", shouted the patient in room 477, delivering a swift kick to Sheldon's chest, knocking him down and the breath out of his body. As Sheldon laid on the padded blue floor, choking, and embarrassed the patient quickly jumped up and thrust his left elbow into Myrtice's mouth. "You fat white bitch! I can't wait to get my hands around your neck and choke the shit out of you!" Myrtice landed on the floor with a loud thud, yelling and screaming for Big Rich and Mr. Gunner to stop the patient. The patient turned and kicked Big Rich in the back of his right knee, sending him tumbling to the floor. The patient then proceeds to lay a flurry of fists to Big Rich's face until Mr. Gunner came and grabbed him from behind. Mr. Gunner picks up the patient, slams him against the wall, and charges towards the patient. The patient manages to get on his feet, delivering a punch to the stomach of Mr. Gunner, followed by a knee to his face. As the four attackers laid moaning on the floor, the patient in room 477 sees that the door to his room is still open! His opportunity; the opportunity for freedom to escape from this hell hole awaited him just a few feet! He jumps over his fallen enemies and dashes to the door. As he gets out into the hallway, he quickly looks in both directions, unsure of where he should go! It's been thirty-two years, seven months, and four days since he's been allowed to come out of his room, and the building was unfamiliar to him.

Crazy how he'd kept up with the days of solitude; hell, it wasn't like he had anything else to do in this box he called home. He quickly makes the decision to go right, as the end of the hallway shown visible light. As he jogs around the corner, the sirens started blaring. Shit! He knew what that meant! Escaped patient; the patient realized that all staff have been alerted and that the local police have been called. He'd been told of many other patients that have tried to escape- and the fate that awaited them once they had been captured. He knew he had to be cautious- one wrong move and he was heading to 'The Abyss'. Turning the next corner, he slows down as he comes upon the guards' station. Half of the wall was a glass pane and, he could see the guards' security table. The televisions and cameras captured the entire building, the patients' room, and every room in the hospital. He saw the television where the camera recorded his room. The fat nurse was the remaining person on the floor, struggling to get up. The patient quickly dropped down to the floor on his stomach. He wasn't sure if there was anyone in the security room but he wasn't taking any chances of being seen. He started pulling himself, body flat down, across the floor in front of the window, turning around every few seconds to assure that no one saw him, and avoiding lifting his head too high. It seemed like he was belly crawling for eternity, feeling his knees rub against the cold concrete floor. As he came close to the corner of the other hallway, he heard a door slam close! Making sure he wasn't in front of the guards' room, the patient in room 477 jumped up, back against the wall. He slid around the corner to the right. Peeping around the corner, he continued his journey to freedom. He ran down the dark stairway, nearly pummeling into the steel door, sweat pouring from every inch of his body. He was in pain, from his heart trying to escape the chest wall. His attempts to turn the door knob with his slick hands were halted by the sounds of two ladies coming in his direction! Dang!, he thought to himself. What was he supposed to do now? As the voices grew close to him, the patient in room 477 began to panic. He looked to his left and noticed a small crawl space between the stairs and the wall. With no hesitation, he jumped over the stairwell, crunched his tall body frame into the crawl space as much as he could, and held his breath. Fear quickly took over his body, mind, and spirit as the two ladies neared the stairs. They stopped to check their surroundings. *"Did ya hear? The crazy dude in room 477 went Kung-Fu on the nurse and orderlies, and now he's escaped. I hope we don't see him"*, said one of the women. *"I should have never taken this job. My husband tried to talk me out of getting a job here"*, said the other woman nervously. *"I heard about that crazy man in room 477 also. How he raped and killed his own* sister, dumping her body into the lake behind his parents' house! How that man didn't see the electric chair is beyond me", said the second woman. "What!" You can't be serious! said the first woman. I heard that it was his brother that committed those heinous acts but the crazy man took the blame for it. What I heard was that their parents forced the crazy patient to take the blame for it so his brother wouldn't have to go to prison. "I guess the older brother was their favorite, and they would do anything to protect him, but they say the older brother ain't wrapped too tight in the head, and the family has been keeping it a secret for years." "Yeah",said the second woman. "I heard that the older brother was hell on wheels; always causing trouble, obsessed with harming animals- just straight psycho. The parents refused to believe that anything was wrong with him and would always defend him. But the one that's in here now? The parents just blamed all of the *family problems on him!*" The patient from room 477 began to rock back and forth, feelings of guilt, regret, and abandonment flowing into his body. How the hell these people knew about him and his family? His brother? The brother he would always protect. The brother he would always take the blame for when he got into trouble. His brother ...his brother.....his brother! The more he thought about his childhood, how it was ruined by his brother's antics, the feelings of guilt and regret melted away. He became enraged! His fucking brother should have gotten the electric chair! Unfortunately, the life of a black person in Dover, let alone anywhere else, was worth less than the three-fifths compromise in The Constitution! Damn! It pained him to think of what his ancestors endured in the Un-United States of Amerikkka, of what he's enduring now with these same racist ass white folks! What his own family put him through in the past!

Unable to control his rising anger, the patient in room
477 jumped up and over the stairwell and glared at the
two women who were midway down the stairs. The
women screamed for help as they attempted to run up
the stairs. *"Too late for you now! You should have
taken your husbands' advice to never work here!"*,
growled the demon-possessed patient as he grabbed
both of the women by their hair and slammed them into
the steel door. *"You got 1.5 seconds to open this door
right now before I snap your damn necks!" "Please
mister, don't h-h-urt us, please. I'm opening the door
now! Trudy, shine your light from your phone on the
lock"*, stammered the first woman as she fumbled for the
right key. As the lock to the door was lit, the second
woman, Eliza, entered the six digit pin number onto the
electronic keypad, inserted the key and unlocked the
door. The patient pushed the two women aside and
flung the door open. The bright sun blinded his vision

so hard he lost his balance and tumbled down the outside stairs, hitting the rubber mat. He laid there, in the fetal position, quickly attempting to numb the pain so he could continue his flight to freedom. After allowing his eyes to adjust to the sun that he hasn't seen in years, he slowly rose up and looked above his head at the two women he viciously slammed against the door. They hurriedly closed the door as he dashed off in the direction of what looked like a driveway going downhill. He'd hope that was the way out of this dungeon he called his prison since he was seventeen. Thirty-two years of living with an inconceivable sin that he didn't commit. The thought of his parents, brother, family, friends and church members brought about an anger so powerful that he couldn't contain. He fell to his knees, and cried aloud to God. *"Why God, why? Why didn't you come to my rescue? Why didn't you help me in my time of need? Why"*? Then, he quickly snapped back into reality. There must not be a God. The God he thought he knew wouldn't allow him to suffer continuously for something that he knew he didn't do. He wouldn't allow such evil to take place in this world. After coming to the conclusion that God wasn't real to him, he got up and continued his journey. He noticed that the driveway lead to a dead end, so he turned to the left, still hearing the emergency alarms and sirens ringing in his ear. The sounds of the police and barking dogs sent him scurrying into the maintenance garage, where he managed to find a hiding spot behind stacks of plywood leaning against the wall. He peered out of a crack of the window to assure that no one was in his sight. He looked out the window, plotting his next move. He could see the gate to the hospital was open. He also saw a maintenance cleaning golf cart parked next to the gate. If he could muster up the strength to run to the cart, jump in, and ride his way to freedom, then his own life would be back in his hands. After looking out of the window, he peeked around the plywood to assure that he was alone. He cautiously made his way to the entrance of the maintenance garage and bolted towards the maintenance car. Wow! Someone actually left the keys in the ignition. As the patient turned the car key on, he suddenly felt what he thought was a torch of fire hit the back of his neck! *"We got him, boss! We got the would-be escaped prisoner!"*, yelled Mr. Gunner. The voices of the people surrounding the patient in room 477 drifted into his subconscious, and eventually, he was totally unconscious. Standing above the limp patient were the adversaries he'd overpowered in his room for a moment, Dr. Jayesh Bhamra, and Jacob, whom Big Rich was holding by the collar of his shirt. *"See what you did, you little punk! You weak, puny nigger!"*, snarled Dr. Bhamra, glaring at Jacob. *"Being so kind and generous* doesn't get you nor these psychopaths cool points here at Healing Minds Mental Hospital. And besides, it's against the rules, MY RULES. You don't know what we do to disobedient people around here, especially unruly niggers like this patient and you? Well, you're about to find out! Drag this patient to 'The Abyss' now!" screamed Dr. Bhamra. "And as for you, my little sneaky do-gooder, I got experimental plans for you. Take him to my office, Big Rich. Tie him up, and leave him there until we take care of Mr. Runaway here!"

CHAPTER 15

The patient in room 477 was positioned in the middle of the 'The Abyss', the dismal torture chamber that delivered the harshest, inhumane punishment to those who dared bucked the system of obedience. The blackened space housed torture objects that rivaled those used in the Medieval Times and slavery. A malicious array of facial masks that bore long, sharp pins, ankle and wrist restraints attached to remote controlled electrical shockers, and skin penetrating rods, whips, and chains lay on the long, wooden table. Myriads of plank tables used to stretch the limbs of the body were sprawled on the other side of the room, waiting for their unsuspecting victims of rebel. In the middle of the room, with arms dangling from the ceiling with shackled legs stretched to the maximum with chains arising from the floor, hung the rebel from room

477. Stripped naked of his clothing, humility, and pride, the patient's mouth was stuffed with a foam ball dipped in chlorhexidine and formaldehyde. His battered body displayed bruises, footprints, and cuts the orderlies and Myrtice delivered to him after the electrical shock rendered him unconscious. And sitting in the corner of the room, behind an immaculate cherrywood desk, sat Dr. Bhamra. He is the evil mastermind behind the horrendous conditions at Healing Minds Mental Institute. He was paid millions of dollars by the state of Delaware to provide care and mental assistance to the inhabitants of the hospital. Unfortunately, Dr. Bhamra and his cronies have been pocketing the money for themselves. The patients live in dilapidated conditions, conditions that have been unknown to the public for years. Patients are beaten, berated, starved, and punished for the mundane of things. They are heavily sedated to keep their minds in psychedelic moods. They

suffer harsh experiments from Dr. Bhamra and his medical staff. Family and friends rarely come and see their loved ones, and for the ones that do, the patients are threatened with a visit to 'The Abyss' if they ever uttered a word to the outside population on how they truly lived. Staff members are not allowed cell phones and security is as tight as Fort Knox. Consequences for loose lips from staff? Termination and blackmail for them as well as their family. Dr. Bhamra rises from his chair and slowly walks towards the helpless patient in room 477. Other physicians and nursing staff, including Myrtice, came into 'The Abyss' to assist Dr. Bhamra in the punishment of the patient. Big Rich pushes a large cauldron filled with wood. He douses the wood with ignition fluid, sets the wood afire, and places the cauldron under the private area of the patient. He points to Dr. Negron, who pushes a button on the wall. The patient's legs are spread as wide as they could go.

He then pulls a lever down, which lowers the patient until his delicate manhood comes close to the smoldering heat and ashes from the cauldron. *"Not too far, Dr. Negron. We're not trying to castrate him just yet- maybe next time, if there is a next time"*, snickered Dr. Bhamra, along with his satanic staff. Sheldon walks along the table of horror, admiring the many items of torture readily at his disposal. *"I'm thinking of giving this boy an electrifying whooping that he'll feel for life!"* Sheldon walks towards a long, wooden box. Unlocking the box, he pulls out a whip. This whip wasn't like anything that has ever been seen before. It was seven feet long, extremely heavy, and made of several braided leather strips. These strips also had titanium strips enveloped around them. The handle of the whip came with a three-prong attachment. An electrical cord was fastened to the attachments and the cord was hooked to a steel box that delivered up to

15,000 joules of electricity. As Sheldon positioned himself to deliver the tortuous lashes, Mr. Gunner comes alongside him, pushing a barrel of water. The lights were turned on, along with the steel box. As the crowd of onlookers stared at the patient in room 477 with malicious glee, tears poured out of his eyes. He knew what was coming-he's been through this before. His only wish right now was for death to come upon him. Death was a welcoming peace compared to the hell he's been through in this god-forsaken institute; he couldn't take life on this earth anymore. *"Let the entertainment began, Mr. Gunner!"*, shouted Sheldon as the crowd of staff cheered him on. Mr. Gunner grabs a large pail, draws up cold water out of the barrel, and sprays the backside of the patient. The water drips down to the cauldron below the patient's private area, sending hot ashes into the room and onto the patient's penis and testicles. As the patient moans, Sheldon points to Big Rich, who presses the green button on the steel box. Sheldon twirls the whip around with such force which made Mr. Gunner duck out of his way. He then brings the whip towards the already-battered back of the patient in room 477. Crrr-aack! Sizzle! The sound of the whip and electrical jolt made the patient's head shake violently as he tried to release a screaming sound muffled by the ball stuffed in his mouth. Three more whips to the back of the patient produced an outpouring of blood and exposed flesh. As the staff laughed, shouted, and high-fived each with with ominous excitement, sparks were flown from the electrical whip and the patient's tattered back. They cheered Sheldon the hero and prodded him to deliver one more whip to the patient. "*Kill the nigger! Make his blood spill until he dies an agonizing death!*", yelled Myrtice as she hurls a spitball in the patient's eye! The nefarious crowd shouted for death to the patient as

Sheldon looks at Dr. Bhamra for approval. *"Hell, why not. His family hasn't seen him in years. They don't care about him; they don't miss him. He's been nothing but trouble since he came here as a teenager. We'll just tell them he committed suicide. Death to the fucking nigger!"*, said Dr. Bhamra to Sheldon. Sheldon orders Mr. Gunner to drench the patient with more cold water. As the voltage of the box is turned up to deliver the final shock of death, Dr. Negron admonishes Dr. Bhamra and the staff for their behavior. *"Not a good idea to murder the patient- some of you all are still under investigation for the circumstances surrounding Flamin' Felicia and her fetus, including you, Dr. Bhamra"*. He cuts his eyes at Dr. Bhamra, who grudgingly agrees with him. *"No, not this time, Sheldon. Just give him a few more whips and get the other nurses to attend to his wounds afterwards"*. Dr. Bhamra leaves the room, head hanging down, as if he was defeated in his maniacal effort to extinguish a human life. Big Rich drench the patient in room 477 with more cold water, while Sheldon turns up the voltage to the highest setting available. The satanic crowd hoops, hollers, and screams as Sheldon readies himself to deliver one last sizzling whiplash to the battered back of the patient. Boom! The electricity flickers out for a few seconds and comes back on. The bewildered medical crowd began to panic. *"Maybe you have that voltage up too high. Turn it down"*, said Myrtice. Sheldon turns down the voltage and revs the whip up again to deliver the electrifying lash to the patient from room 477. Suddenly, another boisterous boom, followed by another boom, and the tumbling of the east wall from 'The Abyss' sends bricks, concrete, and steel blowing into the room with such force that everyone was knocked over. Panic and darkness enveloped the room as the staff members panicked and screamed their way in the other direction out of the torture room. They all left the patient hanging to die, despite the warning of Dr. Negron. Or so they thought!

CHAPTER 16

Not known to the violent staff members at Healing Minds, Miss Groovy watched in horror as Jacob was beaten by the guards and Mr. Gunner. She watched as they shackled his wrists and and ankles, and dragged Jacob in Dr. Bhamra's office to be tied to a chair. She grieved in silence as they stripped the patient from room 477 of his clothes and sodomized him with an iron pipe before sending him to 'The Abyss' for continued abuse. Hiding in a large, rolling laundry hamper in the hallway, she had a view of the outside where the patient tried to escape. They stripped him naked in broad daylight, on the brutal concrete. They sexually assaulted him. How can people be so cruel and hateful, thought Miss Groovy to herself. She couldn't take witnessing this abuse much longer. For years, she allowed her fear of being retaliated and blacklisted keep her from reporting the heinous acts of Dr. Bhamra and the rest of the administrative and medical staff. She couldn't display too much compassion and care for the patients here, in fear of her own life and that of her family. Well, she thought, the day of living in fear was done! Not only was she sickened by the treatment of the patient from room 477, she was appalled by the treatment of Jacob for his part in doing the right thing for him. Jacob made a sacrifice to show love and compassion to the patients, and Miss Groovy was determined to do the same. After everyone cleared the hallway, she peeked out of the covering of the laundry hamper. She slowly lifted up the heavy covering and climbed out of the hamper. She needed to find Dr. Bhamra's office and rescue Jacob. But she knew she had to be careful- cameras swamped the entire hospital, and security was on full alert. She sprinted down the hallway past the laundry room, made a quick left turn, and bolted into the stairwell. Dr. Bhamra's office was on the fifth floor and she knew she couldn't waste any time getting there. Each step up took her breath away. She'd never realized how truly out of shape she was physically until now. She slowed her pace, but she never stopped until she got to the door that opened to the fifth floor. Catching her breath, she fumbled for her ID badge to swipe the computerized lock to open the door. She had to be cautions- she prayed no one was at the door when she entered. After swiping the lock, she slowly opened the door to give herself a sliver view of the hallway. Good! No one was present, she gleed to herself. She entered the fifth floor and continued on her rescue mission to save Jacob. As she got closer to Dr. Bhamra's office, she could hear Jacob yelling for help. She peeked around the corner, making sure no one was standing in front of the doctor's door. *"Jacob, it's me. You're okay now, you're safe. I'm gonna get you out* somehow. *Just hang on*". Knowing she didn't have keys to the doctor's office, she ran down the hallway to the maintenance closet. Maybe she could find a crowbar or some type of object that would pry the door open. Nothing. "*Shit! What do I do now?*", said Miss Groovy as she began to cry. She felt defeated as she ran back to the doctor's office door. "*Jacob, there's nothing I can use to get you out. It's no use; I don't know what to do now*", said Miss Groovy. "*Listen to me*", said Jacob. "*Go down to Dr. Negron's office around the corner. That idiot never locks his office; I know, I've been in there many times*", said Jacob. "*Now Miss Groovy, I know you don't like guns, but Dr. Negron keeps a 9mm Luger Pistol in his desk. Grab the gun and ammunition, and hurry! You're gonna have to shoot the knob off the door*"! Miss Groovy raced to Dr. Negron's office and did as she was instructed. The thought of holding a gun, let alone shoot one, brought on a bout of nausea. I can do this, she thought, as she loaded the ammunition in the gun as Jacob told her. *"Jacob, move far away from the door as you can. I've never shot a gun before, and I know my aim is going to be terrible"*, said Miss Groovy nervously. *"You'll do fine; just aim for the door and keep shooting until the knob falls off. Okay, I'm away from the door. Start shooting now!"*, shouted Jacob. Miss Groovy aimed the barrel of the gun to the door. Her hands were slippery from jitters, so she held onto the gun as tight as she could. Bang! One shot put a bigger hole in the keyhole of the door. Bang! Bang! Bang! Finally, the knob fell off, and Miss Groovy kicked the door in to find a desolate Jacob, tied to Dr. Bhamra's chair, with lacerations, bruises, and blood covering his face. *"Quickly, Miss Groovy. Untie me and get the handcuff key off the table. I'm sure by now that someone has already heard the gunshots, and they're on their way up here. We gotta get out of here"*, said Jacob. *"Not so *fast*", said Miss Groovy. "*They got our friend, the patient from room 477 in 'The Abyss' doing God knows what to him. We have to save him! We have to do something to help him Jacob. No more being passive. No more running away. You should have seen what they did to him, Jacob. We have to rescue him!*", exclaimed Miss Groovy. "*Okay, I got a plan*", said Jacob. " *We'll get him out of there, then we'll call the police and the news reporters. Someone has to know about the real conditions that are going on here*", said Jacob as Miss Groovy unlocked the last set of handcuffs from around his ankles. They scurried out of Dr. Bhamra's office and ran down the hidden stairwell located behind the maintenance closet. Finally reaching the basement of the hospital, they could hear the sickening cheering from the crowd in 'The Abyss' as the patient from room 477 was getting the electrical whipping of his life. "*What the fuck! Is that electrical sparks I hear?"*, questioned Miss Groovy, putting her ear closer to the wall. *"I'm not sure," said* Jacob, *"But Flamin' Felicia told me about an 'electric whip' that Sheldon used on her years ago. I thought she was just talking crazy, but now I'm beginning to think she wasn't lying after all" "We can't see what's going on in there. Jacob, what is your plan to get him out of there?"*, said Miss Groovy in desperation. Jacob had found four empty glass bottles, fertilizer, and some lighter fluid in the storage room next to 'The Abyss'. He filled the bottles halfway with fluid and fertilizer, and stuffed them with rags. He poured lighter fluid onto the rags and instructed Miss Groovy to give him her lighter. *"Go find somewhere to hide under on the other side of the basement, and keep the door cracked open. I'm gonna blast this poor patient out of here!"* As Miss Groovy ran, Jacob lit the first Molotov cocktail, and threw it towards the wall and ran. As the lights flickered and the room filled with smoke and fire, he could hear the bewildered voices of the staff from 'The Abyss'. He hurried back to the slightly damaged wall and lit another Molotov cocktail again, and a third one, dismantling the wall to rubble. He prayed no one saw him as he ducked behind a barrel in the basement. He took out the lighter after he heard the crowd leave 'The Abyss'. *"Miss Groovy, where are you"*? *"I'm over here by the door, Jacob. I'll open it again. I didn't want those devils to see the outside light"*, said Miss Groovy. She opens the door, and they turn to see a visual that would forever be etched in their minds. The patient from room 477 bore the physical and emotional torture that was delivered to him at the hands of the satanic workers. Still dangling from the ceiling, he was unresponsive, bleeding from his electrical-induced lashes on his back. The cauldron of hot ashes still burned from underneath his private area. Miss Groovy immediately burst into tears, while Jacob mustered up the strength to not allow his stomach to come out. The room reeked of burned human flesh, along with the smoke from the cauldron. Regaining her composure, Miss Groovy used her lighter to locate a flashlight. She found the lever that holstered the patient from room 477 in the air and pulled it down. Jacob pushed the heavy cauldron away and began to unshackle the patient's ankles and wrists from the chains. Miss Groovy found a sheet and they both placed the patient on the floor. They attempted to revive the patient by throwing water on his face, but to no avail. *"Call 911, Jacob,"* said Miss Groovy. *" I don't know about you, but at this point I don't give a damn about losing my job. This man is human and he deserves to live. All of these patients deserve better care, and I'm going to tell the public about the conditions in this hell hole"*. Jacob nodded in agreement and placed a call to 911.

CHAPTER 17

"Hello? Hello? Is anyone here? What's going on here?" Thomas walked onto Kimbrough Street from the alleyway behind Freida's Ice Cream and Treats. The silence was deafening, as Thomas stood in the middle of the dark serene black historic district. He was puzzled and scared at the same time. Thomas had gotten a text from Jasmin telling him to meet her in front of Freida's, she urgently needed his assistance. Now she wasn't nowhere to be seen; is this a trick that was being played upon him? Thomas wasn't the type of person that like surprises. His fear started turning to anger as he turned to walk back to the alleyway to his car. Suddenly, Kimbrough Street became illuminated with fireworks lighting up the dark canvas of God's sky. The high school band played Kurtis Blow's 'Basketball' with such jubilance that Big T began to groove to the old

school classic himself. Children walked the streets displaying the intellectuals of the past in pictures and those of the present. Everyone was dancing in the streets, celebrating the crowning of their king, Thomas Darnell Jenkins, as the new forward for the University of Tennessee Volunteers. Thomas' family, Bumble, three of his teammates, as well as Jasmin, was coasting along in his classic Chevy Impala, waving and giving their congratulations! *"Yeah Big T, you made it! You made it to the University of Tennessee!"*, yelled Bumble. He threw a new Tennessee jersey and a hat to Big T. *"Go ahead son, put it on! I'm so proud of you, we're all proud of you"*, gleed Robert. He attempted to jump out to give his son a hug but the car sped up too quickly for him to jump out. *"How in the hell did y'all get in my car? I parked it behind the alleyway!"* Thomas, thinking he was going crazy, dashed to the alleyway, only to notice his car was indeed gone. Damn, I'm straight trippin', thought Thomas to himself. No one, not even his father, told him that he'd gotten accepted into the University of Tennessee. How did this happen? Did his father and godfather use their connections? He didn't even sign a commitment letter! Damn, life is good, exclaimed Thomas to himself. I am the shit! I can hold my own and still have the greatest connections in the world at my fingertips. As the crowd of young, old, men, women, and children exclaimed love for their beloved king of Dover, Thomas began cheering along with them. Finally! His time had come. All of his hard work and perseverance paid off! As far as he was concerned, he was unstoppable. As Thomas gloated down the street, stretching his arms wide, marveling at his kingdom graveling at his feet, his mind ascending into Cloud Nine, and the crowd kept calling his name. *Big T, Big T, Big T* was the chant that echoed in his mind and resounded over and over again with every beat of his heart. He'd pump his fist with excitement while the girls at his school swooned him with kisses and marriage proposals. He gave Jasmin no thought, as she looked on from his classic car with scorn. His friends stood by with envy, but Thomas didn't care. He didn't give a damn about anyone at that moment but himself; not even his own brother. Big T considered himself to be the greatest, above anyone else, even his own father. Thomas continued to gloat in his newfound fame, becoming unaware of the sudden confusion surrounding him. The cheers from the crowd suddenly turned into jeers. Thomas was abruptly startled at the change of mood; he thought for a second that he was walking on air- except that, he wasn't. The bullies from Jackson Rolle High School that interrupted the kids' basketball practice had lifted him up in the air and hoisted him towards his car, throwing him in like yesterday's trash! *"No more glory for you, my nigga! I'm the King of Dover now!*" The jerk that hit him in the face with the basketball sneered at Thomas, looking down on him as his buddy threw another basketball in his face. Thomas attempted to get up, but his body felt more like two hundred twenty tons instead of two hundred twenty pounds. Dead weight encased his entire body as the vicious crowd, which included his family and Manny, descended upon Thomas laying helpless. "*I told you ego was going to be your downfall, Big T; now look at you- you're a pathetic waste of a human being!*", laughed Jasmin in his face as she and Bumble shared a hug and a compassionate kiss. The shock of seeing his crush and his best friend kissing was too much for Thomas to take. He mustered up the strength to sit up in the car and attempted to throw a punch in Bumble's face. Unfortunately, he didn't connect; for his fist was stopped by the one and only Jayla, who was hell bent on getting revenge for their mini showdown. Flurries of

basketballs smacked Thomas all over, and each bounce
left Thomas feeling desolate in this cold, cruel world.
*"Stop! Please stop! I don't know what I've done to
deserve this, but please, I beg all of you- stop!"*, Thomas
shouted. The more Thomas pleaded for them to stop,
the more the crowd mocked their so-called hometown
hero!

CHAPTER 18

"You're a disappointment, a failure, just like your damn father!" yelled an older man Big T didn't recognize. Abruptly, the attention now focused on Thomas' father, who became the next victim of the town's hall of shame. As the crowd began to cower upon Robert, Thomas tried with all his might to pull himself off the floor of his car. *"Leave my dad alone, you muthafuckers! I'll kill all of you if you lay a hand on my father!"* But the crowd didn't listen- they began to deliver the same thrust of basketball hurls at Robert. Big T, still struggling to shake off the dead weight that was holding him down, began to cry at the sounds of his father pleading for mercy. Thomas fought his way off the floor and onto the back seat of his car. Reaching under the seat of his car, he pulled out a baseball bat and jumped out to rescue his father. The rumbustious

crowd became maniacal, hearing a voice that Thomas had never heard in his life before. *"He's mine! Back off Robert! That fucking coward ass dog is mine!"* The crowd went into a frenzy as the unfamiliar person (to Big T) suddenly swooped upon a defenseless Robert in the middle of the street. *"No Pilo! I'm sorry, I'm sorry, I'm sorry! Please don't harm me! Please don't kill me! I have a family! Please, please, please!"* *"You left me without a family, punk! Now it's your time to be away from your family- permanently!"*, taunted Pilo. *"I have no family, no life left worth living, Robert, and it's all because of you!"* Pilo and the crowd became viciously rowdy, barraging Robert with balls of fury, fists of flurry, and words that cut so deep even God himself wept for his minions that he created. Big T tried to fight off the crowd to rescue his father. He was kicking his aggressors, cursing them and God for leaving him in this situation! *"Big T, stop man, damn! What the fuck you doing? Man, what's wrong with you?"*, yelled a familiar voice. *"You trying to kill me! You trying to kill my dad! All because we made it and you didn't."*, screamed Big T as he continued to fight his enemies. Thomas was sweating profusely, thrashing incessantly, and he began to cough up red, foamy blood. Splash, splash, splash! Thomas yelled in agony as three large buckets of freezing water drenched his entire body. " *Big T, what chu' talkin' about? Made what? Man, you buggin for real for real."*, said Skully. In an instant, reality struck Thomas like lightning. He was only dreaming. Forget that, this was the worst nightmare I've ever had, he thought. He sat straight up in the back of his car, jerking his head from one side to the other, looking crazed and perplexed. The angry crowd? They were gone. His family- his father? Nowhere to be found. Pilo? He still didn't know who this person was that his dad was so outspoken about. And the night sky? It was bright, sunny, and as clear as daytime could get. And his friends? Only two were hovering above him in the front seat of his car, looking just as stupefied as Thomas. *"Damn Big T, what's gotten into you lately? You been acting' strange like a muthafucka!"* said Skully, with a look of confusion. *"Why y'all hate me? Why y'all attacked me and my dad? Ya'll tried to kill us! Why man, why?"*, said a dejected Thomas as tears began to fill his eyes. *"Attack? Kill? Thomas, you trippin' big time homey!"*, said Bumble. *"Nobody was trying to kill you and Mr. Robert. We'd never do that kind of junk to ya'll. Hell, you like family to me- sometime, ya'll the only family I got'*. Thomas, still in disbelief over the events that just happened, got out of his car, took his wet and bloody shirt off, and browsed at his surroundings. He wasn't on Kimbrough Street. Hell, he was still in the same spot that he was in last night- on Rollins Avenue, in front of his barber's shop.

Not knowing what was going on or what he needed to do, Thomas slumped to the curb, placing his head in his hands, rocking back and forth. *"Man, I'm tryin' to tell you two Negros, I was being attacked, along with my father, right in front of Freida's place. I parked my car behind's Freida's to meet Jasmin, only to have the whole town cheering, then jeering, then ya'll rode in the parade in my own car....and Pilo....and the basketballs, and them flaw niggas from Jackson Rolle....then.....then....".* Bumble and Skully looked at each other, then looked down at their rattled friend! *"Big T none of that shit happened! You were having a dream! Me and Bumble were walking by and saw your car and we heard you screaming for help",* said Skully, placing his arm around his friend for comfort. *"Big T"*asked Bumble, *what's really good with you lately man? You've been buggin hard. You hardly hang with me and the crew; you haven't been answering your* *phone; you've been walking around school in a daze, like*

you high or something. And all of us been talking 'bout

yo' game. Man, you slipping, you ain't been playing to

your greatest. Are you hurt? Did you hurt your body

during practice? Jasmin told me she heard some niggas

from Jackson Rolle High jumped you down at the

community center. Is it these same cats that Baptiste

trying to replace us for on the team? Man, even yo' pops

came by my house yesterday yelling at me, asking me if

I had you doin' drugs? Everyone's noticed a change in

you T, and it ain't for the good. What's bothering you

homie?", asked Bumble. *"Yeah"*, said Skully,

"Everybody talkin', whispering, saying slick shit about

you and your fams lately, man. Said yo' pops got some

secrets or some shit he been keepin' on the down low for

years. Please Big T- talk to us! What's going' on

witchu?". Thomas looked up at his friends, feeling the

weight of the world on his shoulders. He knew he

wasn't okay but he was hesitant about telling his friends about the troubles of lately. But he knew he couldn't keep hiding from it any longer. Tired, exhausted, and desperate to release his burdens, Thomas finally revealed to Bumble and Skully about the knuckleheads in the Crown Vic; the incident at Peak Ridge; his father's affair with Jayla; his run in with the jerks from Jackson Rolle; his argument with Jasmin and the terse moment with Jacob; his frustrations with Manny not getting his medicine; his fear of Dr. Crumbly calling CPS on his parents; his father's insistent of this Pilo person that seemingly ruined his life, and the pain from Peak Ridge that seemed to never end. Skully's jaw damn near hit the ground, and Bumble's eyes grew in astonishment to the words from Thomas' mouth. *"T*

why didn't you tell us about this a long time ago! Them same niggas tried to run me over when I was walking from my grandma's house one night. I think these niggas somehow connected to them fools from Jackson Rolle that Baptiste done went and recruited. My dad may be a drunkard, but he told me before my freshman year to watch for Baptiste. He said Baptiste was a backstabbing, Sambo, tap-dancing ass Haitian, and according to what I heard, these boys from Jackson are from the same village from Haiti that he grew up in! To tell you the truth, Baptiste has always had it out for you since y'all squared up two summers ago at the Belham County Basketball Tourney. People always said the only reason he kept you on the team was because yo' pops donated money", stated Bumble. *"But for real for real, bro; you do need to go to the doctor, get yourself checked out, and leave whatever pain pills you been taking to relieve yourself. Whatever they are, they got yo' whole mind fucked up!"*, said Skully. *"Yeah, y'all right. I'll go to the doctor- I'm just afraid that he gon' tell me I can't play. That will really mess up my chances to play college basketball'*, said Big T. *"Don't worry 'bout that shit! Your health is more important- besides, you basically got University of Tennessee in your back pocket. If yo' leg got cut off today, they'll still sign you nigga- that's just how great of a player you are", said Bumble. They all shared a laugh and fist bumps as Bumble and Skully helped Thomas to his feet. "Bumble, follow me to Big T's house. T, I'll drive you home in your car- you ain't in no kinda shape to be getting behind the wheel noways".* As they walked to Thomas' car, Bumble's curiosity got the best of him. *"Aye yo T, whatchu been taking' anyways for the pain? Whatever it is, I don't want no part of it, especially if them meds gon' have me hallucinating, having nightmares and shit!"* Thomas reached in his back pocket, removed his wallet, sat back down on the curb, and opened it, pulling out a small plastic zip bag filled with sixteen "Blue Diamonds", the same pills he scored from Chief, his barber, a few months back. Skully examined the pills, and immediately snatched them from Thomas. *"Big T, what the fuck you doin' with this shit. Damn man, no wonder yo' mind been fucked up lately!"* Skully proceeded to take a lighter out of his pocket to set the meds on fire when Thomas snatched his stash back. *"The hell you mean, Skully! These pills are harmless. Yeah I may have been taking more than what I should because my pain been that daggone bad, but I swear this legit from Chief. He would never ever sell me anything that would hurt me!"* Bumble looked at the pills and shook his head. *"You buying these 'Blue Diamonds' from Chief?"*, he asked. *"Yeah"*, said Thomas. *"He said these are prescription pain pills that he gets off the black market from some suppliers in New Jersey."* Skully got in Thomas' face and looked dead in his eyes. *"Man, you don't know shit! You ain't heard 'bout this mess Chief be selling? These ain't no pain pills! This that Molly and Meth shit that don't come from no fucking New Jersey! They come from somewhere out in Nebraska. It's known around here that Chief be dealing with some crackers that come here every month, lying to people about these pills being painkillers. Too many people done got messed up over them. As a matter of fact, this that same shit that our classmate, that white girl Tawny mama got her head fucked up on. Now I heard that she in some kind of looney bin hospital over in the next county!"* Shocked by the real revelation of the pills, Thomas tried to get up to Chief's barber shop to confront him, only to find that the door was locked. Chief was long gone, and that he was too weak to do anything. The two friends helped Thomas walk to his car, with Skully getting behind the wheel. *"I don't know what's going on Big T, but somebody got it out for yo' ass man!"*, said Skully. *" I sure do believe all this drama that's happening' to you got something to do*

with Baptiste and them new players from Jackson Rolle.
Only time will tell'. " *I don't know*", said Thomas. "*But*
whatever is going on, I'm gonna settle it, once and for
all! I'm tired of it. Somebody real deal trying to hurt or
kill me, and I ain't going out like that!'. "*Strange shit*",
said Bumble, looking over at Chief's barber shop. "*That*
fool was opened early this morning when me and Skully
rode by. Chief ass don't never close his barber shop at
12:00 on a Saturday. I bet that nigga knew you was out
here about to die the whole time- and he didn't give a
damn!"

CHAPTER 19

" Skully, you just passed Wicker Avenue. Turn around and go back- I betcha Chief down there somewhere!", said Bumble. *"I know. I'm trying to find another way down Ghost Alley so we can sneak up on Chief without him seeing us"*, said Skully. The young men had abruptly dumped their plans to take Thomas home and instead decided to give Chief an epic ass whoopin' for leaving Big T to die. Riding in Skully's car they recruited their other friend, Noble, to join in on the brutal festivities. Thomas, still reeling from his near-death experience, laid in the backseat, trying to cope with his withdrawal symptoms. *" Just hold on, Big T. Everything gon' be alright"*, said Noble, while he attempted to keep Thomas cool and hydrated. As they came back to Wicker Avenue, Skully took a left and began to slowly creep up on Ghost Alley, infamous for

drug dealing, abusing strung out junkies looking for their next high, and other types of underhanded activities. Skully decided to park in the back of an abandoned house that had a tall, white picket fence. *"Stay here and lay low, Big T. We're gonna close this gate so that no one sees my car. Then we gon' run up on Chief ass. I don't even want him to know you're still alive, let alone see you"*. Thomas agreed and laid down on the backseat, still feeling weak and sweaty from the killer drugs. After closing the gate, Skully, Bumble, and Noble started walking towards Ghost Alley. They could hear the legendary Bob Marley's 'No Woman No Cry' blasting from Pete's Jamaican clothing store, The smell of curry chicken, pigeon peas, fried plantains, and dirty rice mentally tempted their sensory palates and their stomachs. *"Man, I'm hungry"*, said Bumble. *"Me too"*, said Noble, *"but we not here for that now. We gots to get that fake ass barber for trying to kill Big T."* The boys slowed their pace as Skully stopped and asked a group of men standing in front of the Jamaican store for Chief's whereabouts. They pointed around the corner towards the pool room. "Stay woke, my brothas; y'all know Chief stay strapped!", said one of the men. The boys took heed to the warning and proceeded with caution. After they passed the store, they walked further down Ghost Alley until they caught a glimpse of Chief's pearly white BMW i8. Fancy car for a barber, the boys said amongst themselves, having full knowledge of the real cash flow of Chief's livelihood. Coming closer to the pool hall entrance, they quickly ran and hid on the side of the building. Chief's right hand man and security, Bigga Bones, was manhandling a customer that owed Chief money. *"Shit, now what, Skully? We can't let that fool see us! How we gonna get past Bones to see Chief?"*, asked Noble nervously. *"Man, don't start acting like no scary bitch now. Just wait!"*, whispered Bumble. As if the Lord answered Noble's prayers, a ruckus down from the pool hall got the attention of Bigga Bones and some other people. As the pool hall crowd ran towards the new scene, the teens snuck inside the pool hall. The smell and thick smoke of reefer hit them like a ton of bricks. Adjusting their vision to the darkness of the room, the boys proceeded to look for Chief. One of the patrons, smoking the longest blunt ever known to man, pointed to the back, as if she knew whom they were looking for. Walking down the hallway, they could hear Chief's voice, along with- wait- was that Coach Baptiste thick Haitian accent they all recognized? What the hell he doing here, Noble, Skully, and Bumble questioned amongst themselves as they ran into the back room, peeking at Chief and Baptiste sitting on the covered patio. "*Baptiste! You should have seen that nigga screaming and gyrating in his car, like he was having a seizure and shit! Man, that was funny as hell. Me and my crew got us a good laugh offa that!*", laughed Chief as he took a puff of his scented Cuban cigar. "*The only reason his ass still on the team is because of Qualm, but not for long. Once I put a bug in Qualm's ear that his star athlete been using drugs, Thomas' future basketball career is over! Qualm don't even know about my Haitian boys I got from Jackson Rolle to come and play basketball, and it better not get out how much we paying them either, Chief. I got a lot riding on this deal, and I need you to come through*", said Baptiste. "*I'm still pissed at Thomas for running up on me two years ago when he found out I was supposedly bothering them underage girls at the basketball tourney*". "*Nigga, you was fucking them young girls, and you got caught slipping*", said Chief. "*One of them girls you screwed was Thomas' cousin. I found that out later on. That's why he put them hands to you ass, and you know it Baptiste*". The boys were reeling in anger, listening to the ominous conversation. This had been a set up all along. *"Damn, I knew it! I knew Baptiste been out to get Thomas but I didn't know why! Now we know"*, whispered Bumble, and he proceeded to go out and deal with Chief and Baptiste himself. Noble jerked Bumble back. *"Not yet, kid! Just keep listening, then we all go throw them 'bows at these fools"*. As the conversation kept going, Chief and Baptiste were greeted by four boys already familiar to Thomas' friends- but never seen until now. Takeout, Augustin, Pierre, and Julien joined the two men, and they all greeted and conversed in their Creole language. *"I didn't know Chief was Haitian"*, said Skully, scratching his head. *"He always repped Jaimaican and that Rastafarran shit"*. *"Man, who knows what the hell he is"*, said Noble. *"All I know is I'm ready to kick some Haitian and Jamaican ass for my boy Big T"*. *"Baptiste, my coach, my nigga! We think your plan worked after all. Once that white boy Qualm gets word about Fake T's drug use, he'll kick his ass off the team for good. Then University of Tennessee, here I come. Them crackas at Jackson blackballed me every year since that coach found out I was pumping his snow white daughter. No coach nor recruiter would even look my way. Now, one down, and three more flunkies to go!"*, gleed Takeout as the group nodded in agreement. *"So, how we gon' get rid of Bumble, Skully, and Noble?"*, asked Chief. *"I got the perfect plan for them three. Just stay woke and take my heed. I'll give more info about that later once I get in contact with Dreadhead about his two cousins that should have taken Thomas out at Peak Ridge"*, said Baptiste, rubbing his hands in evil delight. The three teens hiding in the room behind their adversaries sunk to the floor in fear. *"What did Baptiste mean by that? Is he trying to kill us like he tried to have Big T killed? I ain't goin' out like that.*

Time for me to start strapping my heat!", Bumble muttered in anger as he and his two friends looked at each other. *"Keep cool, Bumble"*, said Skully. *"I got a plan. But first we need to get back to Big T and tell him everything. Next, we gotta get Big T's car from in front of Chief's shop. I'm gonna create a diversion, making Chief and Baptiste think that someone found Thomas unconscious and called 911. Then, Imma get to Mr. Qualm and tell him everything about Baptiste underhanded dealings. Don't worry, we gon' get back at Baptiste, Chief, them lazy fucks from Jackson, and them two druggies that tried to run over you and T. Ain't nobody takin' a damn thing from us!"*. As Noble and Bumble snuck out of the room ahead of Skully, Skully took one last look at the murderous crew on the porch, put his plan into play with a couple of texts, and ran out behind his friends.

CHAPTER 20

Miss Groovy and Jacob sat in the break room downtrodden, crushed over the recent events at the mental hospital. The staff, lead by the treacherous Dr. Bhamra, managed to cover up the entire incident with the patient from room 477 when local, state, and federal authorities and government agencies conducted their investigations. They managed to lie to the few families that questioned the conditions of their loved ones. The hospital only got fined for not providing care to the patient from room 477 in a timely manner. A measly one thousand, five hundred dollar fine for delay of care. Other than that, nothing, absolutely nothing. Not even the statements and interviews from Jacob, Miss Groovy, and another staff member who dared stood up against the regime that terrorized the patients could convince anyone else about the horrible conditions at Healing

Minds Institute. Sheldon, Myrtice, and Big Rich waltzed into the break room, singing and cheering amongst themselves. *"So you two snitches thought we were gonna get shut down. Ha!"*, yelped Myrtice as she proceeded to bend her fat rear end in front of Jacob's face. Before Jacob could even utter a word of repugnance, Miss Groovy kicked Myrtice dead in her ass, causing the nurse to hit the ground. *"How dare you, give your fat ass over to Jacob to kiss!"*, yelled Groovy as she delivered another kick to the back of Myrtice. Sheldon grabbed Miss Groovy by her arm, and Jacob quickly jumped to his feet, hitting him in his head with a chair. As the two men attempted to lunge at him, Jacob pulled out a knife from his back pocket and swung at them. *"Try it if you want, ya bunch of crooked goons. I'll kill both of ya asses"*! *"Fuck you punk, you won't do shit!"*, yelled Big Rich. At that moment, Dr. Negron bursted in the break room. *"What's going on here! All of you need to calm down, and I mean it! We*

barely escaped being shut down and charged. Everyone,

stay calm and lay low. Jacob, give me the damn knife

now. And no more from trouble from you nor Miss

Groovy." "But she was the". "Jacob, just give him the

knife and let's get the hell out of here", interjected Miss

Groovy. Jacob reluctantly turned over the knife to Dr.

Negron. He and Miss Groovy headed out of the break

room and down to the kitchen. *"Thanks for your help*

Groovy, I appreciate it. I swear Myrtice gonna make me

strangle her one of these days". "No problem, Jacob",

said Groovy, *"But we can't keep using our anger to get*

back at these incompetent idiots here. We need to be

smarter than them. Now Dr. Bhamra told the

authorities and government agencies that the patient in

room 477 didn't have any family. I just don't believe

that. If that's the case, why do they keep his medical

records, his chart hidden. And what about Flamin'

Felicia? What the hell happened with her? We need to get to the bottom of these shenanigans". "*I agree, Groovy", said Jacob. 'The first thing we need to do is to try to find their medical records. And I know that there has to be recordings of everything that's been happening here, especially the torture of the patient from room 477. Let's head to Dr. Negron's office. I'm sure we will find something there. I stole a key just in case he's starting to lock his office now".* They discreetly made their way to Dr. Negron's office. Surprisingly, it was still unlocked, despite all of the recent events. Peeking his head in, Jacob motioned for Groovy to enter. They began to rummage through his drawers, files, and computers, trying to find any information on the patient from room 477 and Flamin' Felicia. Nothing was found on them, but they did discover hidden records of other atrocities that were occurring at the mental hospital. Patients being overmedicated; experimenting new drugs on patients without their or their families' consents; neglect, abuse, and starvation of patients by the staff- the list was never ending. Miss Groovy made copies of the physical papers while Jacob stuffed the USB drives in his pocket. Groovy, searching in the closet for evidence, stumbled upon a hidden panel covered by Dr. Negron's graduation gown from Cornell University. *"Jacob, I think I found something. Come help me move this wooden panel quick!"* As they removed the panel, they laid their eyes on a large, silver, locked box. They took the box and exited out of the office. As they headed to a location to uncover the contents of the silver box, Jacob darted away from Groovy and headed towards the stairwell. *"Jacob, what are you doing"*?, questioned Miss Groovy. *"Just follow my lead"*, said Jacob. Jacob ran up to the eighth floor, with Groovy lagging behind. Entering the floor, they walked to Dr. Bhamra's second office. *"I'm gonna see if*

Dr. Negron's key card can also get into Dr. Bhamra's office", said Jacob. "*You better not do that; what if Bhamra catches us in the act*"?, warned Groovy. "*Not a chance- Negron made Bhamra take a leave of absence after nearly exposing this cesspool*", said Jacob. Jacob swiped the key card three times-finally, the door to Bhamra's real dungeon was opened. Inside the office was things imaginative of anything worse that what those kids saw on 'A Nightmare on Elm Street". Mannequins with knives stuck in them; taxidermies of various animals adorned the dark walls of Bhamra's office. Human and animal brains encapsulated in glass bubbles. Jacob and Groovy shuddered at the horrid site- Dr. Bhamra is a real live crackpot they said amongst themselves. Groovy glanced over to the left side of his office to see surveillance of all of the rooms in the hospital. She went over, looking for anything of value, and she hit the jackpot! Underneath the table was a box filled with DVDs of all the recordings of the events of the mental hospital. As they gathered more evidence, they were suddenly jarred by the sounds of voices in the stairwell. Panicking, Groovy hurriedly grabbed the box and ran out of the office to the opposite end of the hallway. "Jacob, let's get the hell out of here. No telling what they might do to us if we get caught. As Jacob ran behind her, he tripped on the rug in the middle of the floor. He attempted to straighten the rug when he noticed a large, oval ring hanging onto a latch in the floor. What's this, Jacob thought to himself as he pulled on the ring. It opened to a hidden compartment, filled with the medical charts of the patient in room 477 and Flamin' Felicia. Hearing the door to the stairwell open, Jacob grabbed the charts and other media, closed and covered the hidden compartment, closed Bhamra's door, and hid in the closet, praying that whomever was outside wouldn't enter the office. Sweat and palpitations took over Jacob's body as he heard the voices of the security guards nearby. *"Did you hear somebody up here?"*, asked one of the security guards *"Yeah, I saw that crazy doctor's office close but I'm not trying to find out who's in there"*, said the other guard. *"I know what you mean. At this point, I don't care what happens to the medical people here. This floor gives me the creeps. We shouldn't even agreed to come check things out up here, but I know Big Rich will have our hides if we didn't". "I don't care what nobody says, after everything that's happened, I'm not gonna be working here too much longer"*, said the first guard. *"I hope that young kid orderly and that cook don't get killed for snitching on the staff. Man, let's go. We'll just tell Sheldon and Big Rich it was one of the new security guards that was up here and didn't know the rules"*, said the second security guard. When the men left, Jacob texted Miss Groovy to meet him at her van outside of the kitchen facility. After hiding their stash of evidence in Groovy's van they, went back to work, trying to behave as normal as possible.

Hiding in Jacob's chill spot behind the boiler room later on, the pair got on their laptops and began to view the contests of the DVD and USB drives as well as the paper records on hand. There it was, in horrendous plain view, was the recording of the punishment dealt to the patient from room 477. Jacob could barely watch as Groovy's eyes filled with tears. They viewed rapes of female patients, including that of Flamin' Felicia at the hands of Big Rich. They saw patients being held against their will as Myrtice and the doctors inject them and stuff their mouths with god knows what. They even saw previous beatings of the patient from room 477. Hours and hours of abuse and neglect were too much for Jacob and Miss Groovy to handle. But the prized possession came from Jacob out of Bhamra's floor. *"I got* the medical books for the patient in room 477 and *Flamin' Felicia*", Jacob said. Groovy's big eyes grew wider. "*OMG Jacob, that's exactly what we've been looking for. I wonder what they are really hiding*"? They began to read the patient from room 477's chart. The revelation, the shock, the utter appall of the life of the patient came into full view, and now they understood the reasoning behind the patient's erratic behavior, sudden outbursts, violent acts and tendencies, and they reasoning why Dr. Bhamra was determined to have the upper hand on the patient. Towards the end of the medical chart, Jacob and Groovy gasped and nearly fainted as Jacob read the demographics of the patient from room 477. "*Patient in room 477; real name is Morris 'Pilo' Jenkins. Father- Albert Jenkins; mother-Dorris Hamilton Jenkins. Age of patient entering Healing Minds Mental Institution- 17. Reason? Convicted and sentenced to a mental hospital for life for* the rape, sodomy, and drowning of his 12 year old sister Miranda Jenkins. Other siblings- Patricia Jenkins, sister; Gloria Jenkins- sister; Albert Jenkins, Jr.- brother; Isaiah Jenkins- brother; Robert Jenkins- brother". "*What!*", yelled Groovy. "*Robert Jenkins, as in the famous former NBA player Robert Jenkins? Dang Jacob, my brother knew him, and he always stated that Robert was a strange kid and that his brothers and sisters would always get in trouble for his shenanigans. Their parents always took up for Robert and always held him in high regard? Why? I don't know. Maybe they knew he was their meal ticket out of Dover*". "*Hold up, Groovy; I met this man's son, Thomas*", said Jacob. "*They call him Big T, a big time basketball player and destined to be famous like his dad. Me and him almost got into a fight a couple of months ago when I went to visit my good friend Jasmin. He's cocky and arrogant as fuck! I hate him so much!*"

"Jacob, calm down, this is not the time to get into your feelings", said Groovy. "I don't know why they haven't been here to see Morris but they have to know what's really been happening to him here. Since no one is allowed to care for Morris but Myrtice, Big Rich, Sheldon, and the doctors, they don't even know if he's alive or dead. It's important that they get this information about him, and it's up to you to tell them". "Me? Why me?", asked Jacob. "Jacob, I'm counting on you to do the right thing. Please, put personal feelings to the side and let this family know what's going on. Talk to Morris' nephew Big T; the father may not be receptive to you, especially since you and his son don't run in the same circles. I'm gonna alert the authorities again; hell, I may even send this stuff anonymously to the news media. These people have to be exposed once and for all!". "Jacob! Groovy! Where the hell are you two?", shouted Myrtice, shining a flashlight. The pair suddenly became silent as Myrtice made her way into the boiler room. They quickly hid their treasure of evidence, managing to sneak out of the hiding room and out of the exit door that led to the maintenance car garage outside. They each jumped into separate maintenance cars and ducked down as Myrtice and Dr. Negron stood outside. *"I know those two troublemakers are up to no good. We need to find them- and fast, before they get a hold to stuff that could put us away for life!"*, said Dr. Negron. *"Knowing that weasel Jacob, he probably has already found the records of the patient in room 477 amongst other things". Do you still leave your door unlocked Dr. Negron? I'm quite sure by now that snoop has been in your office!"*, Myrtice grunted. The doctor immediately turned paled, radioed for security to search for Jacob and Groovy, and ran up to his office, with the nurse waddling behind him. After the coast was clear, Jacob and Groovy ran back to the hiding spot, gathered their evidence, left the hospital, and went their separate ways, vowing to never come back!

CHAPTER 21

"Alright cats, lets' runs these drills again! And I will not move to the second part of the training until everyone is unison. Concentrate on yo' game and get it right!". The tryouts for the upcoming basketball season were under way, and many of the familiar players were obviously pissed at Coach Baptiste. Noticeably absent were Big T, Skully, Bumble, and Noble, their starters who were supposed to be there. Now the court and team were being taken over by Baptiste's Jackson Rolle recruits- Takeout, Augusten, Pierre, and Julien. When the news broke out that Big T was kicked off the team for violating the substance abuse policy. it sent the entire school body reeling. Many people were shocked, and for good reason- they never known for Big T to be a drug user. And apparently, Skully, Bumble, and Noble were also kicked off the team after testing positive for

marijuana in a random drug test that even had Mr. Qualm, the Athletic Director, questioning the validity of the results. As the boys ended their third set of drills, Takeout took the to floor and commanded everyone's attention. *"Listen y'all, this flow is wack as hell! We really need to find our rhythm and get things going the way that it should be, right coach?* Baptiste nodded in agreement. *"The flow wouldn't be whack if we didn't have y'all sorry, thieving, conniving ass fuckboys from Jackson Rolle here to begin with!"* yelled Mason. *"Who the hell you think you talking to, lil' string bean?! We can square off right now homie!"* screamed Julien as he his three friends charged at Mason. All hell broke loose as the other boys rushed off the sidelines and began tussling. Baptiste and the other assistant coaches ran in and broke up the fight. *"That's it! I'm tired of the bullshit. Let me say this once and for all- Big T, Skully, Bumble, and Noble are no longer part of the team, and I hope that's understood. For those who can't accept it, there's the door- leave right now!'* Baptiste shouted. *"Let's play a quick game. Mason, you the captain of one team and Pierre, you the captain of the other team"*, suggested Takeout. The teams were picked, with the four Jackson Rolle rejects being on the same team. The small crowd inside the gym became larger as the students and staff curiosity became too great to ignore. The boys from Jackson Rolle were actually pretty good, some people agreed. There were even some cheers, but more boos than cheers. Takeout gave Mason a run for his money, bobbing and weaving, faking out Mason as he took a step back and swooshed a three pointer. As the new recruits gilded back and forth on the court with grace and ease, they began to get more support from a once seemingly hesitant crowd. Baptiste's ego swelled with every basket made from his new recruits. There were still a few dissents from the forever loyal fans of the original Middleton High School Boys basketball team. Fifteen minutes into the game, and the team lead by Pierre was killing Mason's team by twenty-five points. The game came upon a break; Mason and his team, feeling the sting from the new players, were hurt and embarrassed by their high school cheering for the new boys in town. They huddled and agreed to continue to play the game, coming up with new plays to overtake their adversaries. The third quarter begins. The jump off begins with Mason getting control of the ball. As he dribbles his way down the court, he takes note of the three goon blocking his every move. He keeps a cool head and manages to make a pass under the legs of Julien to Skip, one of the few freshmans that was moved up on the varsity squad. Skip switches up his position on Takeout, faking a pass that would have even impressed The GOAT himself, Michael Jordan. Takeout trips on his own feet as Skip nets his own three-pointer.

The crowd at Middleton goes frantic as possession switches to the other team. Pierre makes a pass at Julien, only to have the ball stolen by Mason. He runs in hot pursuit down to the goal to attempt a layup, and then‑ what? It can't be! Was Mason's imagination getting the best of him? No‑ hell no! Mason's spirit soared and his smiled brightened like a clown as he passed the ball to his homie, his childhood friend, the one and only‑ Thomas Durrell Jenkins, better known as Big T. Big T roared onto the basketball court like a lion, and made a clean jump shot for the two point play. The crowd went into a frenzy as their true hero, their friend, the real one that should have been on the team finally made his way back home‑ on the varsity basketball team. Takeout, Julien, Pierre, and Augusten stood in the middle of the court with dropped mouths and wide eyes. They looked over at Baptiste, who was just as confused by his scrawny, perplexed look. Then,

Baptiste's entire face fell to the floor at the site of Bumble, Skully, and Noble running onto the court with Big T. What! Baptiste thought Thomas was still in the hospital sick from his near death experience. Well, that what he was told by Thomas' parents and Qualm. What's he doing here? Why is he here? Baptiste looked over at his recruits with disdain. Deafening screams, cheers, and loud salutations echoed from the gym crowd as if this scene was a real live basketball game. Skip, along with three other players, exit the court so that the Fanatical Four could show the Jackson Rolle losers how to really play basketball. *"Kick some ass my niggas"*, said Skip as they greeted their comrades with hugs and high fives.

They joined Mason on the court, huddled for a second, and motioned for Takeout's team to come get their asses delivered to them. Baptiste fervently blew this whistle. *"No, no, no! Get off the court right now.*

You not part of the team anymore, you drug addicts. Now get off my court, out of my gym right now! I run this show, I run this show!" Big T got up in Baptiste's face. "*Make us, with yo' wanna-be sneaky, slick ass! I know all about you and what you've done!*". He then walks over to Takeout, who is incensed with anger. "*You trying to take my spot, my glory, my scholarship to the University of Tennessee nigga! I'd like to see you try it! Game on muthafucka!*", Thomas screamed as he threw the ball into Takeout's chest. "*Square up, y'all Haitian Sensations! Let's get it, right here, right now!*", echoed Bumble, revving the crowd into a whirlwind of craziness. They go for the jump shot; Noble snatches the ball and takes a wild drive down the court, dribbling, shuffling, and shifting from one side to the next. Pierre became confused as to what Noble's next move would be. "*Naw nigga, don't be looking crazy now! I don't know what kinda ball you play but you ain't got shit on me*". He jumps as if he's about to go for a shot, only to land and pull a fake play, passing the ball to Mason. As Pierre scrambles to get back on track. Mason was already at the goal, thrusting a slam dunk that sent the crown hooting and hollering like never before! As Takeout brings the ball to the half court, Thomas squares off directly with him. The boys never take their eyes off of each other, feeling the aura of enmity, treachery, and straight-up hatred filling their close atmosphere. Every crossover Takeout made, Big T was in unison with him. Takeout taunted Big T with talks of his fat, black mammy; retarded-ass ESE brother, and NBA-failure sperm donor. He even spoke about a potential date with Jasmin, the girl "Big Tittie Thomas would never bang". Thomas' rage grew, but his focus on guarding Takeout never wavered. He gave Takeout the workout of his life; every move Thomas made wore Takeout out, making his vulnerability more inevitable. As they passed the halfway line, Takeout was becoming impatient with Big T. Damn, this nigga better than Baptiste made him out to be!, thought Takeout to himself as he struggled to find a way to get past Thomas. He could hear Pierre and Julien yelling for him to pass the ball, but Takeout's ego got the best of him. Like Thomas, Takeout knew all eyes were on him, and he selfishly wanted to make a memorable shot at the goal himself. Thomas glared at Takeout, then formed a mischievous smirk on his face. *"So how did Baptiste pay you to come play here?"*, taunted Thomas *"Was is it money? Or was it in the ass? As in, you and yo mama's naked asses bent over for him?"*. Those words were enough to send Takeout over the edge, as he threw the ball and lunged at Big T. Thomas took full advantage of Takeout's vulnerability and grabbed the ball, giving Takeout a savage ankle-breaking crossover. As he sprinted, Thomas could feel the ante of the crowd as he laid eyes on Bumble. He passed the ball to Bumble; Bumble passed the ball to Skully; Skully passed the ball back to Bumble and Thomas went all in for the alley oop! The play was epic; the crowd went hysterical as they all ran on the court, celebrating the return of Big T, Bumble, Noble, and Skully. The other coaches tried to quell the crowd, but to no avail. Baptiste scolded his new recruits on the sidelines, all in the view of the Athletic Director, Mr. Albert Qualm. Taking in every moment of every player and Baptists from his seat on the bench, Mr. Qualm rose and walked towards Thomas and his friends. He whispered to Thomas, and he and the boys left their classmates and walked over to where Baptiste and the Haitian Sensations were standing. Baptiste, still cocky as ever stood over the five-foot eight Mr. Qualm, but Qualm would not be intimidated. Mr. Qualm took out several pieces of papers out of an accordion folder and handed them to Baptiste. Baptiste read the papers, looked at Qualm, and shrugged his shoulders. *"And? What is this? I don't know why you're showing me these papers for."* *"Did you not pay these young boys behind you to come and play here, Baptiste?"*, asked Qualm. *"I already told you Qualm. These boys transferred from Jackson Rolle. They live here in Dover, they are legally allowed to play here. They only got moved up on the varsity squad when those four loser behind you got kicked off the team for violating the substance abuse policy".* *"Hmm....not according to a very reliable source!"*, shot back Qualm. He turned around and motioned for Principal Rucker, who was standing at the entrance of the gym, to join them. As she walks towards them, she is joined by detectives from the Dover Police Department, and another student⁻ Dreadhead, the one sitting in the cafeteria when the team first got news about the Jackson Rolle recruits. *"I'm quite sure you* know this young man, Baptiste. Well, he got caught selling some drug called 'Blue Diamonds' to an undercover officer posing as a student. He gave us and the detective some damning information about your payments to your new recruits, your beef with Big T, your plan for revenge by having him killed from a drug overdose, and fake documents produced by someone who works in a lab saying that Skully, Bumble, and Noble tested positive for marijuana. Consider this your last day as a coach and employee of Middleton High School- get your stuff out of your office. Security- see that he only takes what he came here with- and as for you four troublemakers? You have no position on the varsity squad. That honor will be bestowed back on The Fanatical Four. You will bench ride until I get ready to let you play!". Qualm turned to the four friends. "Thank you for informing me about everything that has been going on. And as for you Thomas? I hold you as *much responsible for making the choice to abuse what you thought were painkillers. I still got my eye on you‑ do not disappoint me again‑ understood?"* Thomas nodded his head as Mr. Qualm walked out of the gym. Skully let out a loud cackle as Baptiste stormed back to his office. *"See Coach‑ I mean unemployed nigga. You ain't the only one who never fails to plan! We set your ass up the whole time, had you and your flunkies thinking that Big T was in the hospital sick, dying. The joke's on you, Baptiste; now I bet your ass won't be laughing in the unemployment line now!"* Skully, Big T, Noble, and Bumble heckled Baptiste and his defunct recruits as they ran out of the gym to continue their triumph return back to the basketball team!

An hour later, as Baptiste was escorted to his car by security, he got into his Mercedes SUV and sped off. He went straight to Chief's barber shop, ran in, and related to the recent happenings to him. Chief became very nervous, which turned into anger. *"So Dreadhead is a snitch, huh? I don't take kindly to rats!"* yelled Chief. *"Fuck that weak link, I told Takeout I never trusted him. But we'll deal with him later,* said Baptiste angrily. *"Big T, Skully, Bumble, Noble, Mason, and Qualm gots to be dealt with right now! This time, the heat gon' be turned up! And I won't be satisfied until I see someone's soul resurrected to Heaven, then Hell!"*

CHAPTER 22

"Dang Jasmin, how many more times do I have to tell you I'm sorry ? I mean come on baby, give it a rest, please!", Thomas insisted as he attempted to give Jasmin another hug and kiss. Jasmin gave Thomas a playful tug, but she still relented. *"Until the end of time Big T! You have put me through so much these past few months- you owe me a million more I'm sorry baby!"* They both laughed as they walked hand-in-hand along the grassy bank of Lake Eola. Thomas and his family were enjoying an unusually cool weekend at his grandparents' home in Millsboro, about 45 miles away from Dover. It was their 65th wedding anniversary, and the elder Mr. and Mrs. Jenkins were celebrating in style. Robert, his siblings, and all of the grandchildren put on an extravagant backyard venue, completed with catered Southern comfort food;a local band that played

all of the classics of the 60s, 70s, and 80s.; a tented backdrop that housed tables adorned with black and gold linen, white and red roses, baby's breath, string lights that flickered throughout the evening; a six foot vanilla cake with strawberry filling and buttercream icing made by the one and only Freida herself, and the joy and laughter that was felt and heard from family and friends that came near and far to pay tribute to their beloved patriarch and matriarch. It was the beginning of March, and Thomas was looking forward to the March Madness High School Tourney in two weeks, and Thomas was in a much better place in life. He was stronger physically as well as mentally, at times. He'd finally made amends with Jasmin, and the two were finally dating. His Thanksgiving and Christmas holidays were nothing but blessings on top of blessings. He'd finally committed to the University of Tennessee; he and his fellow 'Fanatical Four' comrades were back on the team with full clearance, and the team has managed to keep a winning season under the guidance of their new coach, Jerome Baxter. Despite the investigation regarding the Jackson Rolle recruits, the four knuckleheads were back on the team after complaints of racism and discrimination at the hands of Mr. Qualm by the Haitian Alliance and NAACP. They got playing time, but the tensions between the Haitian Sensations and the Fanatical Four still remained. Baptiste suddenly went into hiding after a scathing report shed light on his pay for play of the boys from Jackson and alleged interaction with drug dealers. He was charged with embezzlement , racketeering, and also had charges of sexual assault with minor children. Thomas didn't understand how the judge even allowed Baptiste to post bail, but Thomas wasn't allowing Baptiste's temporary freedom get the best of him. And Chief? All of a sudden his former barber closed his shop, with a sign on the door claiming that he would be in Haiti on a 'family emergency'. He knew that was a lie, but at this point in his life it was not a concern for him. Thomas was excelling on and off the court, making the honor roll again, even getting inducted into the National Honor Society. He still managed to mentor the kids at the Save our Youth Community Center. His schedule was busy, although stressful. Manny was ahead of Jasmin and Thomas, flying his new kite that their uncle Isaac made for him. *"Manny, don't get too close to the water now, ya hear? Thomas- what are you doing? How many times have I told you not to let Manny near the lake! You need to be closer to your brother!"*, Robert yelled, watching his kids and Jasmin from the patio. *"Dad, you need to chill, we got this! Manny's okay, geez!"*, Thomas exasperated. *"I swear he hovers over Manny and me too damn much. He needs to give Manny some breathing room and let him live!"*, said Thomas to Jasmin. "*Aww baby, your father's just being cautious⁻ that's what parents do, especially if their child suffers from autism. And remember⁻ you have to watch Manny when he is near water⁻ autistic children are more drawn to water because water interacts with all of their senses, which can be hyperactive at times*". "*I know Jasmin, I just want my parents to trust me with Manny more, that's all*", said Thomas as he runs ahead to guide Manny and his kite away from the lake. "*Thomas, Jasmin, Manny? Time to come into the tent⁻ we're getting ready to make a toast to the beautiful couple*", yelled Della, motioning for the three to come back towards the house. As they walked up the slight incline, Thomas rolls up the string from the kite onto the rod. He looks down further to the left of the lake only to notice a blue Toyota Camry, maybe a 2000 or 2001, sitting at the embankment near the dock. Thomas didn't recognize the car, but he hoped and prayed that Baptiste and Chief weren't sending any of their minions at him again for revenge. The family gathered in the tent surrounding the beautiful couple. Thomas beamed at his grandparents; sixty-five years of marriage, and still going strong. Moments of nostalgia, coming to his grandparents home along with his cousins every summer brought back fond memories, when life was so simple. Homemade ice cream, trips to the local farmer's market for fresh fruits, veggies, and those huge elephant ears that melted in his mouth. Swimming parties in his grandparents immaculate pool, coming down that majestic water slide. Only thing that puzzled him- he, Manny, nor his other cousins were permitted to go down to the lake. The was the only rule at Grandma Dorris's and Grandpa Albert's house- and that rule was strictly enforced. Two of his older cousins got caught one summer sneaking down to the lake- and they paid for it dearly. Grandpa's belt was as long and as wide as his big hand, and those lashes on their behinds were to be felt for eternity! Thomas wondered if that same rule was applied to his father, uncles, and aunts. Maybe that's why dad was so terse with me and Manny being down at the lake, Thomas pondered. He looked amongst his immediate and extended family. The noticeable absence of Aunt Gloria and Albert Junior- uncle AJ- puzzled Thomas. They, according to his dad, graduated high school and never stepped foot back into their parents' house. They would send their children down for the traditional summer vacation, but they never paid a visit to their aging parents. Thomas questioned his dad about this years ago, and Robert's response- *"My brother and sister are strange people"*. Thomas and Manny only received letters from their estranged uncle and aunt, with gift cards and money orders. As he wondered about their strange behavior, he saw his mother walking towards him and Jasmin. *"Thomas, I need you and Jasmin to go to the dollar store down the road and get some more takeout plates. There's too much cake here, and it will go to waste if left at this house. Your grandparents are not going to finish all this cake*. She gave him money. *"Please be careful and don't drive too fast"*. Thomas rolled his eyes as he and Jasmin went to his car. Jamming to Kendrick Lamar's 'good city', Thomas rubbed his hands across Jasmin's neck. He could only pray that he has the kind of life and marriage with her as his own grandparents had. As they pulled into the parking lot, Thomas noticed the same blue Toyota Camry that was by the dock by the lake. It was parked way over on the other side of them, conspicuously next to the industrial dumpster. Thomas's heart began to race as a look of concern spread across his face. *"Are you okay baby? Is something wrong?"* asked Jasmin. *"Naw babe, I'm okay. I swear, I'm alright. Let's just get these plates and get back to the house, pronto!*". They went in picked up the items, and stood in the long line to pay for them. Jasmin abruptly cocked her head to the right as she saw a familiar person walking outside in front of the entryway. *"Jasmin, what- or who- did you see?"*, asked Thomas nervously. Jasmin began to stammer- *"J-j-j-just stay here, T. I'll meet you outside. Don't worry, I'll be okay"*. Jasmin ran out of the store, leaving Thomas in the line dejected. His instincts were to leave the plates and follow her out, but another associate came and opened the second register to relieve the overwhelmed cashier. An elderly couple let Thomas get ahead of them in the second line. After paying for the plates, Thomas dashed out the door and ran in the direction he saw Jasmin go in. He walked towards her, then quickly picked up his speed when she noticed she was talking to someone in front of the same Toyota Camry he saw at the lake. Getting closer, he still couldn't make out the face, but the fade with the dreadlocks atop the head brought back ill feelings of disgust. Jasmin caught Thomas' stunned looked, and Jacob whirled around to face the same person he nearly got into a fight with. *"Thomas- it's not what you think. Baby calm down, please, calm down. Jacob has to tell you something, and it's very, very serious. You and the lives of your family are all in peril"!*

CHAPTER 23

It took three local men all of their strength to try to pull Thomas off of Jacob, as Jasmin attempted to step in between the hot-headed boys. *"Dammit Thomas, just stop it! I told you that you need to calm down! Your anger is going to get the worst of you one day- maybe even killed"!* A middle-aged Caucasian bodybuilder managed to yank Thomas away from Jacob and led him away from the gathered crowd. *"Man, are you okay? You need to get yourself together now! Someone probably has already called the police, and these racist white folks will kill you or hurt you badly here, and I know this because I'm white and I've seen it myself. Just cool down- I'll talk to the cops if or when they arrive here. I'll divert them away from here- I don't want you to get yourself nor your scholarship messed up"*. Thomas just looked at the man in bewilderment, and suddenly, he broke down crying. His seemingly peaceful world was beginning to crash again. Not again, not again, not again, Thomas kept telling himself over and over, as he sat on the ground, rocking himself back and forth. This shit can't be happening, he told himself, it can't be true. For all of these years, his parents and grandparents had been living a lie. A devastating, deadly lie! He damn near blacked out when Jacob told and revealed to him the medical records of the patient from room 477, who turned out to be Pilo, the same Pilo that Thomas' father lamented about over all of his life. The same Pilo that supposedly ruined Robert's life. Pilo- the uncle he never knew; the relative that has been locked up in a mental hospital most of his life. The uncle that was sent away when he raped and killed his twelve year old sister- the aunt Miranda that Thomas never got to meet. He cringed when Jacob played the horrendous recording of his uncle being tortured and sodomized at the mental hospital. His anger became even more inflamed when Jacob told him that his uncle's condition at the present time was unknown; the only ones that were allowed to interact with Pilo were the same ones that nearly killed him. Thomas and Jasmin's souls burned with rage as Jacob told them about the other patients being abused by the medical staff; Jacob also shared with them about Miss Groovy seeking out the authorities to tell them again about the atrocities at the mental hospital, along with the evidence that they had discovered. Thomas had become so enraged that he'd taken his anger out on Jacob, nearly breaking his neck when he choked him. Now, all he could do was sit on the ground and gaze- gaze at the sky, wondering what kind of god would allow the suffering of innocent people to take place. The tears would not stop flowing; his heart would not stop hurting; and he couldn't clear his head of his uncle and the other patients; his family; the lies; the deceit; the

cover-up; Robert's odd behavior over the years, and

Della's passive attitude towards her family and life

period. Finally getting himself and his emotions back

together, he thanked the bodybuilder for his help and

walked over to Jacob and Jasmin. *"Jacob, I'm truly*

sorry for putting my hands on you. All of this- this

travesty- is hard to grasp. I pray you can find it in your

heart to forgive me; but for now, I have to finally settle

this deceit from my family once and for all'. "It's all

good', said Jacob. *"I just couldn't stay at that dungeon*

anymore, witnessing the treatment or lack thereof that

those poor people were receiving, especially your uncle.

They provoke him a lot, and once he loses his temper, all

hell breaks loose, and unfortunately he suffers for it

later. Hell, any patient there that does something,

even the most stupidest act, is set up for a harsh,

unnecessary punishment'. Jasmin reached over and

gave Jacob a long hug. *"Friend, it took a lot of courage, bravery, and sacrifice for you and your co-worker to do the right thing, risking your careers and your lives. I'm so proud of you. You have come a long way from your rough upbringing Jacob, and I know God has His protection all over you"*. I wish God would have had His protection over my uncle for all these years, Thomas thought to himself. *"What are you going to do now, baby"*?, asked Jasmin. *"What else? I'm going back to the house and confront every one about all of this, including my grandparents. I don't care about it being their anniversary, it's past time for someone to start telling the damn truth"*!, said Big T. *"I'll follow y'all back to the house, so you can have the papers and videos to show to your family,"* said Jacob. Jacob's phone rang. As he walked away to converse with the other person on the line, Jasmin hugged Big T, shedding tears of sorrow herself. *"Thomas, you have to keep it together! You just have to! Manny is depending on you, your uncle Pilo is depending on you, I'm depending on you. Please baby, be calm".* "Jasmin, I'm tired of being calm, but I know I have to be! It just seems like nothing is going right in my life right now. I just wanna". They were cut off by a frantic Jacob. *"Big T, you have to come with me, right now! We gotta get up to the Delaware State Police Department. Miss Groovy has met with someone who is familiar with your uncle, dad, and the situation with their sister all those years ago. We need to go now. You're gonna have to wait to deal with your family".* Thomas turned to Jasmin, who was looking at a message on her phone and was as pale as a ghost. *"Big T, I agree with Jacob. Please to go the State Troopers station now, and be careful on these streets. Not only do you need to find out what really happened with your family, you also need to tell them that Baptiste and Chief have put a hit out on you, Bumble,*

Skully, Noble, and Mason. They broadcasting it all on social media, and I got a bad feeling that they are serious! And apparently, they got their goons, the Haitian Sensations, out trying to hunt y'all down as we speak"!

CHAPTER 24

Jacob kept at the speed limit, as he and Big T nervously looked in front, behind, and besides them for any signs of trouble. The news that Baptiste and Chief have a bounty on him and his friends' head had him livid at first, but now he was scared- for his life and that of his family's. He didn't respond to the texts from Jasmin, who had gone back to his grandparents' house after meeting with Jacob at the dollar store. They all had been demanding her as to Thomas' whereabouts, and Jasmin was wearing thin of consistently lying about the reason as to why he didn't come back with her. He'd had already forewarned Bumble, Skully, Noble, and Mason about their former coach and barber's death threats, and all of them were slated to meet up with him and Jacob at the police station. Jacob slowed into the parking lot of the Delaware State Trooper Department and turned off the car. He looked around for Miss Groovy's van, but it wasn't in sight. Just then a knock on the passenger front window sent both Jacob and Thomas' hearts dropping to the pits of their stomachs. *"It's me, Jacob and Thomas"*, Groovy waved as she jumped into the back seat. *"I hope we haven't been followed by anyone, Jacob. Me and my husband have been getting threatening messages from Drs. Bhamra and Negron, as well as Sheldon, Big Rich, Gunner, and that fat lard Myrtice. One of my neighbors told me today that Sheldon and Big Rich have been to my house several times over the past few days but me and Johnny are hiding out somewhere else. Jacob please watch out for yourself and your family. We know too well that those thugs are capable of"*. She turned to Thomas and they shook hands. *"Nice to finally meet you. Your uncle is in terrible shape at the mental institute, and I can only hope they have not committed any further* atrocities against him. That video of him in 'The Abyss'-". Thomas cut Groovy off. "Yeah I know about it- Jacob has told me everything, and I've seen the horror on the videos myself. I wish there was something I could do to help my uncle". Suddenly, headlights lit up the parking lot. The three quickly ducked down in their seats- all of their lives were in danger, and there was no telling who or what was coming after them. As the car door slammed, Miss Groovy slowly peeked at the officer getting out of the car. "Oh Jacob, that's her. That's the state trooper I talked to when I brought all of the evidence we found in Negron's and Bhamra's offices". Thomas looked up- it was State Trooper Sylvia McArthur- the same officer he'd met at his house after his run in with the goons at Peak Ridge. They all quickly jumped out of the car and called her out. She turned around and immediately used her badge to get into the station. "Quick! Get in here and go all the way *down to the end of the hallway to the last room on the left. Let me get Lieutenant Swackard so I can brief him on everything that's been happening lately.* Once inside the room, the boys and Miss Groovy sat anxiously, waiting for the officers to make their entrance. Trooper McArthur entered the conference room, followed by two fellow officers pushing three carts carrying a total of ten evidence boxes. Lastly, Lieutenant Swackard came in, commanding the attention of everyone in the room. His stature was tall and lean, with a unique mustache with either ends curled upward. He removed his hat and assisted his officers in placing the boxes on the table. Afterwards, he took long, hard stares at Jacob, Thomas, and Miss Groovy. He began to open one of the boxes, viewing its contents, and began to shake his head. *"This case‑ the harrowing rape and murder of Miranda Jenkins on July 15th, 1982, is one that will forever be etched in my mind and my spirit. I haven't eaten, slept,* nor lived a life of quality ever since I, as a young detective at that time, found the wrangled body of that innocent little soul. Thomas, what I'm about to tell you regarding the circumstances surrounding that day is the truth, the whole truth, and nothing but the truth! And I have been living a lie for all of these years, thinking that I could just leave this case and live my life as if I've had no regrets. But I'll tell you, I've had many regrets. I've regretted withholding the real truth for all these years. I've regretted caving in to my boss' demands to assist in covering up the truth regarding your aunt's murder. I've regretted my self-medication with alcohol and prescription drugs to numb the pain of that terrible night. And most importantly, I lost much time, missed many blessings, and and went to bed with my wife and kids every night knowing that I allowed an innocent man to rot in a mental hell-hole for a crime that he didn't even commit".

CHAPTER 25

State Trooper McArthur, the other officers in the room, as well as Thomas, Jacob, and Miss Groovy sat stone-faced as the words of Lieutenant Swackard rolled off his tongue. *"So basically, what you're saying is that Mr. Morris Jenkins, aka Pilo, never committed this horrendous crime?"*, asked Miss Groovy. Her curiosity piqued as she sat straight up in her chair and placed her hands on either side of her face under her chin. The others followed suit, waiting for the lieutenant to reveal what he's been hiding for thirty-two years. Swackard sat in his chair, lit up a cigarette, and looked down at the table with grim. *"Sir?"*, questioned McArthur, *"If Pilo didn't kill his sister, then.....who did"*? Swackard looked up at Thomas with pain in his eyes. *"Thomas, Big T, the real killer of your aunt Miranda was none other than your father, Robert Jenkins himself. And your grandparents, Albert Sr. and Dorris Jenkins, forced your uncle, along with my boss at the time, Sargeant McMasters, to confess to the crime and take full responsibility".* Everyone in the room was taken aback behind the uncovering of the truth. They all looked at Thomas with sorrow and pity, as he never deserved to bask in a life like this. Thomas, emotionally drained and overcome with much grief, was surprisingly not shocked by the news from Swackard. He just sat in his chair, arms folded, forcing and pressing himself to keep his anger at bay. At this very moment, life didn't mean much to him. Everyone that he trusted and looked up to betrayed him. He was taught to respect and hold the police in high regard, but now he sat in front of a so-called decorated thug with a badge who admitted to letting his innocent uncle get locked up for a murder that he didn't commit. He didn't care for anything nor anyone anymore, including his precious brother Manny. Thomas looked at the lieutenant, as if he was waiting for him to continue his story. *"Big T, your father was a very smart, skilled, and talented child. From the very beginning, he excelled in sports, especially basketball. He'd won many tournaments and received much recognition for his moves on the court, especially his famous crossovers. He was destined as a child to be a professional player and your grandparents Albert Senior and Dorriss spared no expense to assure that Robert got whatever he wanted, whatever training he needed to be amongst the best, even at the sacrifice of your other uncles and aunts. Unfortunately, Robert also had an evil persona that your grandparents didn't want the community to know about. Robert was strange, obsessed with harming small animals, fire, and bullying other kids at school. He'd been arrested numerous times in his youth for cruelty to animals. Your grandparents were very good friends with*

Sargeant McMasters at the time, and your grandfather would make whatever sacrifice, whether it be in money or goods, to assure that Robert never saw the inside of jail or juvenile detention. Albert Sr. and Dorris considered Robert to be their meal ticket out of Dover, and they basically neglected their other children to assure that Robert received only the best. His siblings often got blamed for Robert's troubles, and the only one who had the balls to stand up to Robert and their parents was Morris, or Pilo, as you have probably heard your father called him. Your grandparents lashed out at their other children constantly. Morris would go to school with whip marks and bruises all the time, but a blind eye was turned. Robert never learned responsibility and always blamed others for his problems". Lieutenant Swackard went into a box with the number five written on it and pulled out a picture. He walked over to Thomas and handed him the picture.

"This is Robert and Morris' sister, your aunt Miranda. She was nine years old in this picture". Thomas took the photo into his hands. His aunt Miranda was as beautiful as day. Her big, brown eyes were captivating. She had her long, beautiful hair done in pigtails, wearing a red, white, and brown checkered dress with a white bow adorning the collar. She was sitting with her hands folded in front of her, with a wide smile and a picture of a Black Jesus in the backdrop. Thomas put his hand over his mouth and began to cry. Why, how, just why did she have to die the way she did? What did she ever do to my father to suffer his mortal punishment? And how could Albert Sr. and Dorris make his uncle take the blame for his father's transgressions? All these questions lingered in his mind as he handed the photo back to Lieutenant Swackard. *"No son, you keep it. This is probably the only picture of Miranda that exists while she was still living.*

Anyways, Miranda was, as they called it back in my day, mentally retarded. Dorris had a very difficult pregnancy, and little Miranda went for too long without oxygen to her brain. Your grandparents were devastated, and rightfully so. But instead of nurturing her, they neglected her, just like they neglected all of your uncles and aunts. But unfortunately, Miranda bore the brunt of the most brutal punishments by Albert Sr. and Dorris. Not physical, per se, but emotional and chemically. Her parents took her to all types of doctors and psychiatrists, who fed her with harsh, morbid medications that made Miranda very ill. They were determined to make her 'normal' and heal her mind from the 'demons that possessed her'. Unfortunately, Miranda's behavior became more erratic and unpredictable. Robert teased Miranda, and finally all of the other siblings had enough of Robert's abuse. They protected Miranda from Robert, especially Morris.

*Robert would try to repeat some of the doctors'
experiments on Miranda, only to get his ass beat on a
daily basis by Morris. Your grandparents witnessed
Robert doing horrendous things, and they still would
defend him, always saying that 'he's just a boy; he
meant no harm'".* Lieutenant Swackard paused, took a
sip of water, and gathered himself to reveal the next
part of the Jenkins' family secret- the rape and death of
Miranda.

CHAPTER 26

"*Despite being behind intellectually, Miranda was not lagging behind physically*", continued Lieutenant Swackard as the group of officers and civilians listened to his every word. "*She developed physically very early; according to reports from her school teachers, Miranda was the only girl in her class and age group at that time to have breasts. The girls teased her; the boys would run behind her, pull and snap her bra strap, and run off. Miranda was humiliated. By the age of eight, she had run away several times, but not too far; only to the neighbor's house or the farmer's market up the road from your grandparents' home. Robert teased your aunt incessantly, and your brothers and sisters, especially Pilo, would beat up Robert. As usual, Albert and Dorris took up for Robert while your aunts and uncles were* constantly punished. *Now, as much as Robert was as smooth on the basketball court, he wasn't too smooth with the girls. Most of them hated him. They knew all about his love of torturing animals, setting things on fire, and his incessant secret parties he had where he possessed a Ouija board, calling on evil spirits. As Robert reached puberty, his sexual curiosity understandably peaked, and he behaved like an animal, attempting to get any girl to sleep with him. At the age of fourteen, he met your mother, Della Lovelace. Della was a smart kid herself but, and no offense Big T, she was on the heavy side at her age. She was also teased by her fellow peers. I guess there was a rumor going on at the time that Della was willing to 'give up the goods' to anyone, so your father saw his chance to finally lose his virginity. Well, the rumor was false; Della was a good Christian girl who came from a very strict religious household. She was not as easy to convince like people assumed she was. Despite this, Robert actually took a liking to your mother and they started secretly dating. He would never pressure Della to have sex with him, but he still had that desire to be sexual with someone".* Lieutenant took off his glasses as the tears began to stream from his eyes. Everyone else in the room already knew what the next revelation was going to be about, and no one was prepared to hear it. *"When Miranda hit twelve years of age, she was physically shaped and developed like an adult- tall like her parents and siblings, large breasts, big but, wide hips- you get my drift, Big T. God rest the dead"*, said Swackard as his voice began to quiver. Thomas' heart sunk- he wasn't sure if he could even handle the lieutenant speaking about his aunt like this, but he was determined to hear the whole story. *"Your grandparents, aunts, and uncles had went to church that fateful night, all except Miranda and Robert.*

Miranda was very sick that day, and Albert Sr. had Robert to stay at home to watch over Miranda. All of the children protested, especially Morris. They knew what Robert was capable of, and they didn't feel right with their vulnerable sister being in Robert's presence. The parents ignored their children's pleas, of course, and off they went to church. Miranda had just showered, eaten a bowl of chicken noodle soup that Dorris had made earlier that day. Robert gave Miranda her medication, and off to bed she went. Now according to Robert's confession, which was never spoken nor heard of outside of this building, he went into his room, took out some Playboy and Penthouse magazines he'd stolen from the grocery store earlier that week, and viewed naked women. He began to masterbate, letting his sexual desires rise, rise and rise, until he couldn't stand it anymore. He'd called Della and tried to convince her to come over to his house to lose their virginity, but her parents were out on the town, and she had no way of getting to his house. He continued to pleasure himself, until he grew tired. He'd went inside his parents' room and stole a bottle of Jack Daniels' that his father kept in his steamer trunk in the closet. As he drank, his thought process turned to evil intentions, and those intentions were now focused on Miranda. Robert stated that he'd grabbed a flashlight and made sure all of the doors were locked in the house. He'd turned off all the lights in the house, cut the flashlight on, and proceeded up the stairs to Miranda's room. He slowly opened the door, and shined the light onto Miranda, who was in her bed asleep. The breeze outside was cool and crisp, a welcoming feat to the hot days of summer that year, so Miranda had her window opened. She laid in bed with nothing but a bra and panties on, according to Robert. It was unusual for preteens to sleep half naked, but Miranda was sick with the flu, so she must have been very hot that night. He closed the door, covered the top of the flashlight partly with his hand to shine as less light as possible, and proceeded to tip-toe over to Miranda's bed. He said that he stood over her for a minute, 'gazing at her sexiness'. I'm sorry Thomas but those were your own father's words, words that I will never forget for as long as I live. Robert reached out, placed his hand on Miranda' ankle, and moved his hand up along to the bottom of her butt. He carefully placed the flashlight in between her legs, and cautiously slid the crotch of her underwear to the side. He said he placed two hands into her vagina and began to play with her. He said he jerked back a little; I can only assume it was because of his first interaction with the female genitals period". Thomas' eyes became wide, like he'd been ran over by a diesel; Miss Groovy and State Trooper McArthur were crying. Jacob was on the verge of tears as he looked at the pain and hurt on Thomas' face. The other officers were just as stunned as Thomas as one of them asked Lieutenant, how could he hide something so hideous as this? This is not what we officers take an oath for"? *"I know"*, said Swackard. *"Believe me, I have been paying for this inconceivable sin since that grim day, and I forever will be. Well, Robert stated that he removed his clothes and moved in closer onto his sister. He carefully closed her legs so he could remove her panties. By this time, according to Robert, the meds and the extra dose of sleeping pills he managed to crush and slip into his sister's juice had finally taken effect. He spread her legs, looked at her genitalia, and began to masterbate. He pushed her legs even wider as thrusted his penis in and out of his sister- his own flesh and blood".* Big T vomits all over himself at the ghastly thought of his own father's incestrous actions against his drugged up aunt. Thoughts of killing his own sperm donor raced inside his head as he aimed to process all of this madness in his brain. Lieutenant Swackard continued, with swollen eyes from crying himself. *"Robert said he just kept going, and going, and going, enjoying each move that he made with Miranda. As he tried to turn her over, the flash of thunder from the window and the crash of lightning scared him so much he flung his arms to the side, dropping the flashlight on the floor. That's when Miranda suddenly jumped up and bumped into Robert, still kneeling in between her legs. He said Miranda kept asking who was there, who was in her room. It was totally dark, and she couldn't see. That's when Robert said his panic turned in feeling of inferiority. He punched Miranda in the face and pushed her back down on the bed. Miranda screamed and hollered for Robert to come help her- there was 'a very bad man' that was trying to hurt her. Robert stated that he said nothing as he seized her legs high into the air. He tried to put* his penis back into her but he said Miranda fought him off vigilantly, still screaming for him to come get the bad man off of her. Robert said he overpowered her long enough to get himself back into her vagina. He said Miranda screamed and cried and yelled out his name for help as he continuously pounded his penis into her. She continued to holler, trying to wiggle her way out of his grasp. Robert told McMasters and myself he was just about done with his sexual conquest when Miranda suddenly snatched her arms away from him. She managed to grab his face, pressed her thumb into the sockets of his eyes, and scratched his entire face with her long nails. He said Miranda shouted, 'I don't know who you are or where my brother Robert is but when my daddy gets home I'm gonna tell on you! I'm gonna tell my daddy what you did to me, you mean ol' man, and he's gonna have you in a lot of trouble'! Robert said that he yelled at Miranda and told her to shut up. He said *that Miranda jumped up suddenly and asked him 'Robert, is that you? Are you the mean ol'man that just hurt me? That just hit me? That just put something hard inside me? Why would you hurt me, your very own sister? Why?' He said that he tried to calm Miranda down but her screams got louder and louder. Robert said without warning, Miranda kicked him in his chest and jumped off the bed, dashing away from him. Robert said in the darkness he tripped over the flashlight on the floor. He picked up the flashlight and ran after her. He said Miranda running down the stairs, yelling ' Daddy, daddy, please help me! Robert hurt me! He hurt me really bad! I have a bad pain in my private part! Robert hit me in the face. The house was still dark but it was dimly lit by the lightning flashes from the midnight sky. Robert said he chased after Miranda, yelling out at her, telling her he was sorry for hurting her, that he didn't mean to hurt her. Robert said that*

Miranda kept telling him to leave her alone, to stop chasing him, that she was gonna get her daddy on him. Robert begged for Miranda not to tell their father. Robert then revealed to us that Miranda said to him: 'Well, if I can't tell daddy on you, then I will tell Morris on you. Morris always beats you up for picking at me, and I'm gonna tell Morris that you hurt me and my private part. Morris will beat you up; Pilo will beat you up bad, like he always does!'. Robert said at that moment, his fear of his father turned into pure hatred for his brother. Those words from Miranda raged inside of him, and he knew he couldn't let Miranda tell Pilo nor their father about what he had done. Robert said that's when he sprinted towards Miranda and kicked the back of her knee, causing her to hit the floor with a loud thud. He said he proceeded to get on top of Miranda and laid several fists of fury all in her face and chest. He said Miranda fought him; she fought him hard, harder that Morris had ever tangled with him. She managed to push Robert off of her; she jumped up and continued to run away from him. Robert said he chased her into the kitchen, grabbing a butcher knife and a rolling pin off the kitchen counter. Miranda dashed out of the kitchen, then back into the kitchen by way of the swinging doors by the pantry. She opened the door next to the pantry that led to the backyard, the swimming pool, and down to the lake. Robert was in hot pursuit. He said she kept yelling and screaming for help; saying that Robert hurt her; she was calling for her daddy, and she was calling for Pilo to 'come and beat Robert up". Robert said that's when Miranda slipped and fell by the pool. Robert said he grabbed Miranda by her long hair and pummeled the rolling pin several times into her head. She swung her arms with vigilance, trying to fight of her sibling attacker. Unfortunately at this point, Robert had the upper hand and he was going to make sure that she didn't tell daddy, Pilo, nor anyone else. Robert said he picked up the knife and dragged Miranda down to the lake. That's where he hit her some more with the rolling pin. He said he then grabbed the knife and slashed Miranda in her thigh. She screeched so loudly that it caused one of the neighbors to turn their house lights on. Robert said he stabbed, and stabbed, and stabbed her. With each stab, Miranda screamed and yelled for help. Despite her injuries, she still fought hard for her life. Robert said at that moment he was getting frustrated because 'the bitch just wouldn't die'. Filled with burning rage, Robert took the knife and thrust it into her chest. He said Miranda slowly became silent, with blood gushing from her mouth. He then proceeded to throw her face down onto the grassy bank. He climbed on top of her, pulled her head back, and slit her throat from ear to ear. Miranda was dead; she was finally dead. He said he could hear his sister's blood running out of her body. He sat there on top of her for a moment, relishing in his satanic victory. He became alarmed when he heard doors opening. It was the neighbors, and they were making their way to the lake! Robert said he jumped up and dragged Mirando into the lake but she wouldn't sink. Panicking, he grabbed the knife and rolling pin, and ran back up the embankment back into the house. He discarded the items from the kitchen into the furnace in the basement, ran back upstairs, took a shower, and changed the sheets off of Miranda's bed. Robert regained his composure, running out of the house to join his curious neighbors. 'Hey Robert, did you hear those screams'?, asked Mrs. Beasley. 'I will never forget the terror in whomever's voice it was. Me and John were woken out of a deep sleep'. 'I heard the screams, but didn't see anything, Mrs. Beasley, lied Robert. 'Is your father home'?, inquired Mr. Beasley.

'No, sir, they all went to church, except for me and Miranda. Miranda's sick with the flu, and my dad made me stay home and look after her. She's sleep; I gotta go check up on her'. 'Make sure you lock all the doors and windows- and don't let anyone in the house unless it's your parents', admonished Mrs. Beasley. 'I'm gonna call the police so they can come check out things. But I'm not sure if they can; this thunderstorm is fierce, and it may have caused some trees to fall in the road'. Robert ran back in the house and did what he was told. Robert then told McMasters and I that after he locked up the house, he went into his parents' room and climbed up into their rooftop patio. He said he sat on the lounge chair, took out a Playboy magazine, and began to masterbate, all while looking out at the lake, where he had just thrown his dead sister".

CHAPTER 27

Thomas exploded, jumping over the table, lunging at Lieutenant Swackard. *"You bastard! You call yourself a man of the law! How in the world could you have lived with this secret for all of these years!"*, Thomas shouted as he laid his fist right into Swackard's mouth. Trooper McArthur and the other officers jumped onto Thomas and threw him against the wall. Guns drawn, McArthur placed handcuffs on Thomas. *"You, young man, are under arrest! I know you are angry but you have no power nor authority to take the law into your own hands with violence against a law enforcement officer!"* *"Authority?"*, Thomas snorted. *"Your boss here abused his authority by taking the law into his own hands by not arresting the real jackass that killed my aunt Miranda! How's that for power? All of you LEOs are the same- stick up and defend each other, even when you are dead ass wrong!"*. Thomas whirled around and got smack into McArthur's face, staring her down, as if he'd wish his looks could kill her on the spot! Jacob and Miss Groovy stood nervously in the corner, trying to convince everyone to lower their voices and control their anger. *"It's okay, State Trooper McArthur. Thomas is absolutely right. I deserved those words, deserved that knuckle sandwich to my mouth, and I deserve a whole lot more grief, guilt, and punishment that what I've received,* `` said Swackard, as he removed the handcuffs from Thomas's massive wrists. *"But the fact of the matter is is that Miranda did not deserve to die the way she did and her brother Morris did not deserve to rot in hell for thirty-two years for a crime he's one hundred percent innocent of. That's why I'm telling my story- my truth- the real truth, that should have been told years ago. I am determined to right my wrongs that I have done, and get some type of justice and retribution for this poor family, for little Miranda, who should have had a chance at life. Everybody, sit down now, I'm not finished yet".* After they all took in a bite to eat, Lieutenant Swackard dug into another evidence box and took out photos. They were pictures of his pathetic father, with the scratches Miranda left on his face for the whole world to see. Thomas turned his head away in scorn; it was as if he didn't even know his father anymore. Swackard continued- Miranda was *"When the rest of the family returned home from church, Robert was already in bed, and he had made a stuffed dummy to make it seem like Miranda was still asleep. He had locked her door so that their parents wouldn't go in. Miranda, Miranda, are you okay? Robert said he could hear his mother calling his dead sister's name. He got out of bed and went down the hallway to where his mother was standing in front of Miranda's room. He told his mom that she was asleep,* she had taken all of her medication, and to leave her alone. Dorris thank Robert for being such a caring brother and gave him a hug. She retreated to her room as he looked over to his right. Morris, also known as Pilo, was standing in front of his own room, glaring at Robert. Morris felt that he or Patricia should have been the ones looking after Miranda, not Robert. Robert said that Morris walked over to Miranda's room and tried to open the door. Robert said, 'Didn't I just say that she was sleep! Get away from there'. Morris replied, 'Why is Miranda's door locked? You know Miranda hates having her door locked. And why isn't her night light on? I don't see the glare under the door. Miranda's scared of the dark, and you know it. What did you do to her?' Robert stated that he told Pilo he didn't do anything to her and that he needs to mind his own business; he was just jealous that mama and daddy picked him over everyone else to stay home and care for

Miranda. Robert told us that Pilo was persistent and demanded for him to unlock the door so he could check on their sister himself. Robert refused, and the boys got into a scuffle. Their father came out and broke up the fight and made both of them go to bed. The next day, according to Robert, was the end of his existence, as he knew it! He'd woken up to a bloodcurdling scream. The sounds of someone pounding on the door jolted everyone out of bed and downstairs. It was Mrs. Beasley. 'Albert, Dorris, please step outside right now! Something's bad really happened! Quick- down to the lake'! As the three adults ran down to the lake, the other children raced out of the back door by the pantry, nearly beating the adults to the dock. There they were, in plain view- the Delaware State Police Dive Team, the state police boat, other state troopers, county, and local law enforcement, and the ever present media. The entire lakeside community also stood still, watching the fiasco that was going on in their small world. *Not this much excitement has occurred here since the 1960s when the Freedom Riders rode through town for civil rights. Members of the dive team could be seen pulling what looked liked a body to the lakeshore. The body was then covered after numerous pictures were taken by the crime scene investigation unit. The scene was blocked off as me and Detective McMasters made our way to the local citizens to ask any questions. The local law enforcement had approached the Jenkins family, asking Dorris if everyone was accounted for in the family. Dorris stated that everyone was here except for Miranda, whom she told was still asleep in her room, trying to overcome the flu. The children were told to stand on the patio as the parents were questioned. Patricia said in her statement that she had suggested that she was going back into the house to check on Miranda. All of the siblings were worried about her, albeit Robert, who was dribbling his* basketball. Patricia said that she and the other siblings noted Robert's strange behavior, and they all began to question amongst themselves if Robert knew what was going on. Of course, Pilo decided to challenge his brother again. Pilo, in his statement, asked Robert again why Miranda's door was locked and why wasn't her night light on. Pilo said that Robert got into his face and was about to say something when they both paused, and looked over to their neighbors. The boys noted the Beasleys' pointing over in their direction. Pilo said he turned to Robert, and said it was like the color in Robert's face began to fade away. Robert was visibly nervous about something. By this time, the coroner had completed his initial look over, and the body was taken to the morgue for further testing. The crime scene was still being processed as Detective McMasters and I walked over to the Jenkins' house. Mrs. Beasley had revealed to us that she'd seen Robert by the lake late *last night after she heard the screams. We approached*

Mr. and Mrs. Jenkins and told them what we were

informed of, and that we needed to ask Robert a few

questions. They gave us permission to question Robert.

As I walked over to Robert, the Jenkins immediately

took Detective McMasters to the side, which I will admit

was very suspicious. I kept my mouth shut, as this was

my first murder case. I'd taken down Robert's name

and age when Detective McMasters demanded for me to

stop. 'No interviewing of minors without an adult

parent being present- you can't ever forget that,

Detective Roger Swackard!' I gave my apologies to the

Jenkins family. Robert protested, stating that he didn't

know anything and that he didn't want to be interview.

Detective McMasters reminded him that there were

witnesses who saw him at the lake after the screams

were heard and that he could be charged with hindering

an investigation. Robert reluctantly agreed, and went

in the house to change clothes, with Mr. Jenkins following. After Albert Senior and Dorris left with Robert, me and McMasters, the other children stayed behind, with the local police department officers patrolling the home. While we were gone, Pilo had revealed to his other brothers and sisters that Miranda's door was locked and her night light wasn't on last night. Albert Junior rushed up to Miranda's room with the others following him. They all banged on the door, calling Miranda's name, but she wouldn't answer. Isaiah had found an ax and began chopping at the lock. Morris eventually kicked the door in and all ran into Miranda's room and straight for her bed. Imagine the horror when they pulled the covers back and saw that Miranda was not there- only a large, stuffed dummy Patricia used in her Biology class a long time ago. The children screamed as Gloria called out to the officers. They dashed up the stairs, and the siblings showed them *Miranda's bed- with no Miranda. The officers radioed for more backup as Gloria told all of the siblings to get to the garage.* They jumped into the station wagon, and Patricia jumped behind the wheel. They *peeled out and sped up to the Delaware State Police substation in Millsboro, where we had Robert interviewing him. Robert was in the room explaining the reason as to why he was down at the lake when we suddenly heard a commotion in the hallway.* 'Hey, *you're not allowed back here'* was what we heard the receptionist yell. *We heard stomping and* running as the sounds neared the door. *Next thing, the door burst wide open, with the other Jenkins children rushing in at Robert.* 'Where is Miranda? Why wasn't she in her room? What did you do to her? We know you did something to our sister, you murderous piece of shit!' *the children yelled as they began to beat Robert up with sticks, chairs, and anything else they could get their hands on."*

CHAPTER 28

"It took every officer at the substation to get the children under control", continued Swackard, opening his third pack of cigarettes. "The kids had told us that after we left the house, they broke into Miranda's locked room, only to discover that she wasn't there. Dorris fainted, and Albert Senior went into a rage himself, jacking Robert up against the wall, nearly choking him to death, demanding to know why he didn't keep his eye on Miranda? Albert said she'd probably had run away again and begged Detective McMasters to leave so he could start a search party for his daughter. But unbeknownst to the Jenkins clan, McMasters and I already knew where Miranda was. We saw her mangled body on the lakeshore after the dive team pulled her out of the waters. She was nearly decapitated, with multiple stab wounds to her body,

including one large wound to her chest. We'd already knew about the neighbors seeing Robert down at the lake; they had recognized Miranda's voice as the one who was screaming for help. We'd already been told of another person hearing Miranda screaming for help as she was being raped in her own home. The passerby, who was walking home from the local bar, had already identified Miranda clearly calling Robert's name and that she was going to tell her daddy; he heard Miranda telling Robert that Morris was going to beat him up. We'd had already obtained a search warrant for the Jenkins' home after the Beasley's saw Robert carrying some items back into the house; all we wanted was for Robert to tell his side of the story. And it was past time for Albert Senior and Dorris to face the realization of their son Robert- that he was evil; that he was demonic; that he was a failure; that he was a criminal; that he was, simply, a murderer and a rapist; the number one suspect in the death of their precious daughter. But at that end of the day, they were human, with feelings. It was going to be hard to tell them that their daughter was dead; but we knew that time had to come. The other children were sent to the other side of the substation, while Robert and I was placed in another room. McMasters remained in the original room with Albert Senior and Dorris. Tears rolled down Robert's face when he heard his parents scream for Miranda. He'd known that they were told; that Miranda was dead. He sat in the room as they cried unto God to give life back to their daughter. Robert sat for hours and hours in silence, the tears flowing down his bloody cheeks, still scarred from Miranda's scratches. McMasters finally came into the room with the Jenkin parents, and I was told to leave and tell the other siblings the fate of Miranda. Anger, confusion, sorrow, and revenge all set in as the children totally lost their *minds over the death of their sister. Morris was ready to tear down the door again so he could get his hands around Robert's neck. Other officers pinned him and the other brothers, Isaac and Albert Jr. Gloria and Patricia held each other, trying to console a pain that would never go away. It seemed as if that day would never end; the sadness just encased the entire police substation. Cries from even the most seasoned detectives were heard around the building. Everyone knew and loved sweet Miranda. Life was unfair; many wanted to kill Robert himself, whom finally confessed to the events of that night. Hours later, still sitting in the room with the children, we were all shaken to the core as the door flung open. We were greeted with shock and utter disgust as Detective McMasters rushed in and snatched Morris and dragged him away from his family. I followed behind them and demanded to know what was the meaning behind Morris' detainment. After Pilo was slanged into the cell, McMaster glared at me and told me to mind my damn business, or I would be finding my twelve year old daughter floating in the lake nearly decapitated. Scared for my family and their safety, I did what I was told. Next thing I knew, there was a news conference held where McMasters declared that Morris was being arrested and charged with the murder of Miranda; that he'd made a full confession of his crimes, and that Robert was totally absolved of any responsibility. Other officers and I were bewildered at the reveal. A total lie was spinned to make it a public truth, and an innocent kid paid for it. To bring this tragedy to an end, Morris was ruled incompetent to stand trial, and was eventually sentenced to Healing Minds Mental Institute for the remainder of his life. And life went on- McMasters quickly moved up in the ranks of the state trooper enforcement, making it all the way to state congress, where he served a surprising twenty-five years before retiring in New Jersey. I also moved up, becoming lieutenant and will be up for another promotion next year; Robert went on to become a star high school, college, and professional athlete before his career-ending injury; and Albert Sr. and Dorris got what they wanted- a famous son, money, recognition, and prestige- which they never had coming from a family of sharecroppers from Alabama. And the rest of the sibling? Well, I'm sure you found that out at your grandparents' anniversary party tonight Thomas".*

Swackard finished his story, the third pack of cigarettes, and was beginning to open another one when Big T got up and perused through the evidence boxes. Pictures of his uncle's mugshot; photos of Robert's facial injuries; the blood of his aunt on the lakeshore; evidence photos of the knife, rolling pin, and the stuffed dummy found in Miranda's bed; the battered door that his uncles tore down trying to save Miranda; and pictures of Miranda's undergarments. All of Big T's emotions were empty; he was tired, he was mentally exhausted; he was over it until he looked inside the last box labelled 'Coroner'. He opened the box and viewed the most startling pictures ever known to him. Aunt Miranda's body, her dead body, lying on the table. She had been stabbed seventy-eight times; her head was nearly detached from her neck. Her vagina was blacked and bruised from Robert's reign of terror. Her nails bore the blood and skin of Robert's hideous face. Swackard revealed to Thomas that the funeral was closed casket; the mortician couldn't even cover up the damage Robert had inflicted on her. He stared at Swackard. *"That's it! I'm done with this conversation, done with my father, and I'm done with you. I'm taking these photos and I'm gonna confront dad and my grandparents about their skeletons!"* *"Thomas, you can't do that",* said Swackard. *"You can't take state's evidence out of here, or I'll have you-". "You'll have me what? Arrested"?, shot back*

Thomas. "You can't do shit to me that you haven't

already done to yourself". "And besides", stood Jacob. *"I*

recorded your entire confession to covering up Miss

Miranda's murder. Now what you will do is give Big T

exactly what he wants and what he needs. No more

playing games from none of you law enforcement crooks

in here. You all are pathetic; a joke; a blatant disgrace

to the badge you smear on a daily basis. Fuck all of you

conniving, colluding, criminally- infested thugs in here.

Thomas, Groovy, let's get out of here. We still gotta

meet Thomas' friends, and we need to get back to the

mental hell and check on Mr. Pilo. I got a plan to get

him out of there". The three civilians left, with

Swackard, McArthur, and the other troopers staring in

a daze. Finally, Swackard followed behind Thomas,

putting his hand on his shoulder. *"Do what you need to*

do. For once and for all, I got your back. I really mean

it this time. I will not let you and your family down again.". He opened the door, and they all looked at the parking lot, with the shock of their life. Jacob's car was vandalized, with a voodoo doll of Big T depicting a bullet hole in his head. Just then, Skully, Bumble, Mason, and Noble pulled up in Noble's SUV. *"We came earlier and saw them Haitian punks fucking up this car. We got out and chased them but they had jumped into that same car that tried to run me and you over and peeled off,* `` *said* Bumble as he looked at Jacob and Miss Groovy. Thomas quickly introduced them and demanded that they get into the car. *"Jacob, get into the car with Miss Groovy and we'll follow y'all to the mental hospital. We got to bust my uncle out of there tonight! No more games!"* *"Uncle!!!"*, said Thomas' friends in unison. Big T shook his head- dearest to pay for his damn sins"! *"Get in the car, and I'll explain everything. You just don't have a clue how much I've learned about my family history, and it's time for daddy*

dearest to pay for his sins!"

CHAPTER 29

Mason, Bumble, Skully, and Noble, obviously disturbed by Big T's unearthing of his family's demons, were boggled at the utter mess that Thomas' grandparents and Robert had inflicted. *"So, how we gon' get your uncle out of Healing Minds? They got that place locked down like Fort Knox"*, asked Mason. All of them were terrified of being caught, scared of being harmed, and nervous of the consequences of their impending actions. But they knew that this mission was of importance to Thomas, and they were riding with him until the end. Thomas shrugged his shoulders. He called Jacob, who was driving ahead of them in Miss Groovy's van. *"Um, how we s'posed to get up in there? I hope you and Groovy got some plan in place."* *"No worries, Big T. Me and Groovy already know what to do"*, stated Jacob. As they neared the mental prison, the two cars turned a sharp left, getting onto a desolate, clay road that with tall trees on either side that made the night and the planned prisoner escape more eerier. They parked their cars amongst the trees. *"We're gonna have to foot in from here"*, said Groovy. *"My husband and his brother will be waiting for us at the base of the hill by the hospital. We'll sneak in from there. They're gonna shut down the electricity and disable the computers that control the passcodes on all of the patients' rooms. I'll make a diversion with Molotov cocktails. After I set the maintenance garage and laundry room on fire, you and your friends will follow Jacob to your uncle's room in the medical ward. We got two other people on our side inside the hospital that will assure that the door to his room is accessed. They already have your uncle dressed in civilian clothes, ready to go"*. Bumble was skeptical. *"Lady, you sure this plan gon' work? How we can be so sure that them* guards won't try to kill us?" "Chill Bumble. We can't worry about that now! I'm sure you'd want us to do the same if it was your family. Just stay cool, and back Big T, Jacob, and Miss Groovy up", assured Skully. Bumble reluctantly agreed, and the group started walking to the base of the hill. When they arrived, Groovy's husband and her brother-in-law were already there, with all types of gear to initiate the prisoner break. They were given flashlights, along with police batons, baseball bats, and stun guns to ward off their attackers, should the unthinkable happen. Unbeknownst to the group, Jacob had stolen two of Dr. Negron's guns he kept in his office; he planned to use them as a last resort, a very last resort. "Alright, is everyone ready? Everyone know what the plan is? You boys stay close behind Jacob and my wife, got it?" said Groovy's husband to a bunch of nervous wrecks. They understood, and took off to the back of the mental hospital. A wire gate with a lock stood between them and Pilo's freedom. Groovy's brother-in-law removed the lock with a bolt cutter easily, and they ran to the main computer room on the bottom floor, taking caution not to alert any security patrol on foot. The door to the computer room was surprisingly opened, and they all snuck in. John gave Groovy a burlap bag, filled with Molotov cocktails, ready to be lit. *"Take one of the boys with you and head to the laundry room. Once Matt breaks into the computer's security system, I'll send you a signal over the walkie-talkie to start lighting up the gas bombs. And be careful- don't let anyone see you."* Groovy did what she was told, taking Mason with her. *"I bet Baxter's lazy ass fell asleep in his car again"*, said Jacob. *"He always takes his breaks in his car, leaving this door opened. Noble, stay at the door and keep a lookout for an older bald man coming back here."* John and Matt walked over to the mainframe while Jacob and the other boys positioned themselves by the door that lead into the hospital. Matt, a software engineer, sat himself at Baxter's desk and began working his magic. He was able to decode the security passwords, disabling all of the locks of the patient's rooms. Minutes later, an overhead page could be heard calling for Baxter to call the main security desk. *"They know the patients' locks on their doors have been compromised. We better get this show going now! Give the signal to Groovy, John. Everyone else, get your weapons and get ready to follow Jacob"*, said Matt. *"And send that signal to Groovy quick! I see baldie Baxter coming back now!"*, said Noble. John radioed Groovy to light the Molotov cocktails, and they all waited. Four explosions rocked them to the core! *"Hey, that must have been Groovy and Mason, and Baxter just took off in the direction of the laundry room. Let's get shit poppin! We gotta get Big T's uncle out of here"!*, yelled Noble. He shut the back door after John left out and joined his friends at the front door. John, on the outside, gained access to the generator and electrical panel, and shut down the electricity. He radioed for Groovy and Mason to look out for Baxter coming their way. Total darkness enveloped them all, and he could hear the panic and mayhem coming from inside the hospital. On Jacob's signal, Big T and his friends dashed out of the computer room and hurried to the medical ward on the fourth floor, where Pilo's uncle was being kept. They ran down to the end of the hallway and made their way into the stairwell. They got to the entrance to the floor, only to notice that the entry was locked! " *Shit, I forget they still use regular keys to open the doors from the stairwell*", screamed Jacob. *"No worries, my nigga! I got this"*, said Bumble. He reached for his back pocket and pulled out a Luger. He pumped several shots into the lock and door handle until they came off. Hearing screams from inside, Thomas kicked the door in, and they were met with resistance from Sheldon and Big Rich. *"I told you this nigger was behind this, Big Rich",* said Sheldon as he glared at Jacob. *"And it looks like he brought in a couple of more black, poor, dumb nigger thugs to help him".* Skully took a baseball bat to Big Rich's head. *"Cracka, you fuckin' right we black but we ain't poor, we ain't dumb, we ain't no thugs! And we damn sholl ain't nan' one of ya'll niggers!"* Skully shouted as he, Bumble ,and Big T delivered ass whippings powered to them from their ancestors, the kings and queens from Africa⁻ the Motherland, the land of Ogun, who still reigned and ruled Mother Earth! *"Jacob, let's find my uncle now before I real deal kill these got damn saltines!",* said Big T. As the boys ran off, Sheldon managed to trip Skully. Skully yelled for help. The boys turned around to see Sheldon hovering over him with a bat that Skully hit Rich with. Jacob pulled out his gun, shooting Sheldon in his thigh. He ran up and pulled Skully out of Sheldon's path as the racist orderly fell over in agonizing pain. *"Oh, so you came prepared prepared, huh!"* Big T exclaimed to Jacob as they all laughed, heading to the other end of the hallway to the medical ward shouting black power!! A person waving a towel caught their attention. There, in the ward, looking through the glass, stood two male nurses and a visibly weak, desolate, sickened man sitting in a wheelchair. Thomas paused as he stared at his uncle, the man he's heard about all of these years, but never laid eyes on. Pilo's entire life was wasted behind infinite walls of cinder block; years that could never be given back with time. Thomas couldn't begin to imagine the mental state of his uncle Pilo, rotting in prison for life for a crime that he didn't commit. Thomas nearly broke down but his friends held him up. *"I know this is emotional for you Big T, but we don't have much time to simmer around",* said Jacob. One of the male nurses, Tyron, let the boys in. *"My wife has her SUV ready behind the maintenance car to get patient 477, I mean, Mr. Pilo out of here to safety"*, he said. Sad, that majority of the staff never knew Pilo's real name for all this time, Jacob pondered to himself, regretting not saying something about Pilo's treatment way beforehand. Thomas seemingly read Jacob's thoughts. *"It's okay homie; better now than never to do the right thing. Thank you all so much for risking your lives to rescue my uncle"*, wept Thomas. Just then, Pilo aroused out of his drugged up state. *"Uncle? Did you just call me uncle? Who are you?"* Thomas walked to his uncle and gave him a hug that lasted for what seemed like eternity. *"We'll tell you everything later, uncle Pilo. For now, we got to get you the hell out of here"*. *"Hell yeah"*, said Bumble. *"And I do mean now! Those hospital goons heading our way as we speak"*! Just then, a fleet of security guards, lead by Dr. Bhamra and Myrtice, marched their ways towards the prison breakers. *"No way in God's green Earth are you bastards getting out of here with that child rapist and murderer!"*, yelled Myrtice as she instructed the security guards to charge the group. Out of nowhere, Mason and Matt bust onto the medical floor from the stairwell. They threw four Molotov cocktails towards the medical mob, setting some of them on fire. As they began to retreat, Thomas and Jacob ran towards Dr. Bhamra and Myrtice. They grabbed the two demons and dragged them into the stairwell. As the rest of the group left carrying Uncle Pilo down the stairs, Big T and Jacob leashed an ass whipping on Bhamra so horribly serious, they left him unconscious. They hog-tied Myrtice and carried her down with them. They all got outside to greet Miss Groovy. *"Gotta trek a little further; you wife had to move the car when the maintenance garage caught fire.*

Hey, what are y'all doing with Miss Lard here?", Groovy questioned Jacob and Big T. Jacob reached into a bag he was carrying and pulled out pictures of the punishment the staff laid on Pilo in 'The Abyss'. He stuck them under the rope that held her together, along with a bag of USB drives. *"When the authorities get here, they'll get a good look at the abuse you and your minions put Mr. Pilo and these other people through. And don't worry, I made plenty of copies just in case one of your comrades gets to you before the crooked ass police do!"*, snorted Jacob. *"Hey, guess I'm not some cheaply paid, young and dumb orderly after all, you murderous wench"*! Jacob, incensed with anger, began to reach for his back pocket. John grabbed him. *"Don't waste your life on this subhuman; don't become what these people running this place have already done. Let's go!"* The group quickly left, leaving Myrtice on the ground. They could hear sirens coming from the front of the hospital. Screams, cries for help, and total chaos was still present when they finally reached Tyron's wife's SUV. They laid Pilo on soft blankets in the trunk, while Tyron's wife gave him water and food. *"Everybody pile in; I'll drop you off down by the clay road closer to your cars"*, said Ebony. Everyone did what they were instructed, and Ebony cranked up the car. As she sped off, she could see someone in her rearview mirror flagging her down. *"Wait for me, please don't leave me to die here! Stop I say, Stop!"*, said the person running behind them. Ebony slammed on brakes as everyone turned around, staring at the nearly naked woman running behind them. *"Who is that?"*, inquired John as he proceeded to open the door. Jacob's jaw dropped. *"Dang, that's Flamin' Felicia, Licorice, Dawn, whatever the hell she calls herself. I forgot all about her. They've had her drugged up ever since she bit Sheldon in the face!!"*, he said. Groovy reiterated

Jacob's shock as John helped her in the car. The pale Caucasian patient, still sporting the disheveled red hair, squeezed between Bumble and Mason, as Ebony once again took off. *"Thank you, thank you all so much. And I sure appreciate you helping that poor black man that was down the hall from me. I thought for sure he was dead after I heard him screaming for life in 'The Abyss'".* Bumble looked up and stared at Flamin' Felicia for the longest. Then it dawned on him; his eyes grew big as he snapped his fingers to get his friend's attention. *"Oh my God, look who it is y'all! This ain't no Flamin Felicia. This our classmate Tawny mama, Miss Brenda, the one that got sent here after she went stone crazy from overdosing on them 'Blue Diamonds'!"*

CHAPTER 30

Reaching the woods off the clay road, the group of prison rescuers jumped out of Ebony's SUV to collect their thoughts. They were still high on adrenaline and could not stop talking about the prior events. Big T sat next to his uncle, who was still groggy from the medications that Myrtice had pumped into his IV. He turned on his flashlight and looked at the pictures of his uncle from his teen years that he took from Lieutenant Swackard. His physical features favored Robert's in many ways, except that Pilo was lighter than his father. His uncle was tall, lean but muscular in his younger years; now he just looked malnourished, like he barely existed. Saggy bones, no muscle mass, sunken face and eyes; damn, prison literally takes the life out of you, thought Thomas to himself. He then looked over at Miss Brenda, their classmate Tawny's mother. *"Does*

Tawny know where you are?", asked Big T. Brenda glanced at Thomas with sad eyes, and put her head down. *"I don't know to tell you the truth. Her father had me sent to Healing Minds, more like Killing Minds, to rot to death. I'll always remember him telling me that he will make sure that Tawny doesn't see nor know anything about me anymore. Yes, I was a drug addict; yes, I did some bad things to feed my habits, but everyone makes mistakes. I thought that people, especially your own family, was supposed to help others, not hurt them".* Brenda began to cry as Thomas gave her a napkin to dry her eyes. *"Wrongs will be rights soon enough, Miss Brenda. But right now, we got to get you back to your family. Or you could stay with me and hide out; we'll try to figure this whole fiasco out",* said Thomas. Brenda smiled. *"You're very kindhearted; the risk you and your friends, and the few people that really cared about us took, I just wish we all could have gotten every patient out. You have no idea the suffering we have endured over the years under Dr. Bhamra and his goons".* Just then, Pilo began to arouse. Thomas helped him sit up so he could finish eating. He gave Brenda some food also. *"Uncle Pilo, you okay?",* asked Thomas. He put the flashlight to his face and Pilo gazed at him. *"Damn, Robert spit you out, neph! You look nothing like your mother. By the way, how is Della?",* asked Pilo. *"She's probably worried about me. I left grandpa and grandma's anniversary party to get some plates when me and my girlfriend ran into Jacob. He told me you were in here, Unc; what those horrible people were doing to you. We went to the state trooper's office afterwards, where I was finally told the truth about everything from Lieutenant Swackard. Thirty-two years, and it's not right. I hate my father right now. I hate Albert Senior and Dorris right now! How could Robert kill my aunt Miranda, throw her into the lake like trash, and then your parents and the police cover it up, forcing you to confess. It's-".* Pilo cut him off. *"Thomas, I can only imagine how you feel right now, but I've been living this nightmare all my life. Where is Robert right now?"* Thomas answered- *"He's still at your parents' house- I'm ashamed to even say they are my grandparents, and I'm embarrassed to know that Robert is my father! All of this mess is just insane to me. I just-".* Everyone got quiet as they heard a car turn down the clay road. Thomas, his friends, and the rest quickly scrambled inside the three cars to hide. The car coming down the road turned off its headlights as it crept down the dark path. The window rolled down and the driver turned on the flashlight, catching a set of tires in its view. The driver turned off the ignition, got out, and walked towards the three cars hiding amongst the trees. "Hey, whomever you are, come out of the cars slowly with your hands up!" commanded a familiar voice. Thomas jumped out. *"Don't shoot us, Lieutenant Swackard, it's just us"*, said Thomas nervously. All of the other occupants came out as Swackard commanded. Swackard, McArthur, and the other two state troopers Thomas had met earlier withdrew their guns as they exhaled a sigh of relief. *"Listen, you guys better get outta here and fast! There's about to be helicopters and more local, county, state, and federal agents swarming this area. If they see y'all with these two escapees, it's your assess"*, said Swackard. *"As far as I'm concerned"*, he continued, *"I don't really give a damn what happens to me at this point. All I know is that I've finally lifted this burden of guilt off my shoulders. Where is Pilo?"* Thomas pointed to Ebony's vehicle, and Swackard walked over. He turned on his flashlight and laid his eyes Pilo. Although he has aged, Swackard could still recall clearly as day Pilo's sad, brown eyes, streaming with tears as he and other officers watched Morris' mugshot photos taken. Swackard let out a loud cry and fell to his knees. Everyone stood around him, watching him beg God for mercy for Pilo and whatever life punishment he knew he deserved for not doing the right thing. He got up, approached Pilo, and incessantly apologized to him for all of the pain and suffering he had to endure. Pilo, still weak from the meds, shook Swackard's hand, turned over, and went back to sleep. Thomas' disdain for Swackard increased; he was determined to not be so forgiving. *"That's the problem with us black people- we are too easy to be so damn forgiving to our enemies"*, he whispered to Bumble, who nodded in agreement. *"Fuck him, Big T. "Let's peel out now before all of us get shot. Besides, I don't trust these crooked ass cops anyways. They might be setting us up for the kill for real."* McArthur helped Swackard to his feet as everyone else jumped into their cars. *"Thomas looked back at Swackard. "I can't find it in my heart to* forgive you nor my father, but I guess I appreciate your finally stepping up to the plate", Thomas said with half-hearted empathy. "I don't expect any forgiveness from you nor your uncle, and I'm totally okay with it", said Swackard. He shook Thomas' hand and watched as they all got into the car. He walked over to Masons' car and spoke to him. "Take this dirt road all the way down until you see another crossroad of dirt. Turn to the right and keep going until you see a paved road. That's the road that will take you to the Lanape River Visitor Center. Once you get there, then you'll be on your way back to your grandparents' house. Please be quick! I don't want y'all to get caught". They all left while Swackard, McArthur, and the two troopers walked back to their vehicle. Swackard looked at his comrades . "Don't worry you three, I won't involve you in any of this. I'm prepared for whatever consequences of my actions will bring." McArthur shook her head- "Sir, I'm *not worried about my job either. Me and these two guys stand behind you one hundred percent. I'm more worried what Thomas is going to do to his father once he get back to Millsboro. And lest you forget, there's talk about some people looking to kill Thomas and his friends. I think we better follow them, sir. I got a bad feeling someone's gonna get hurt tonight".* The thought of imminent danger to Thomas, his friends, and all the innocent people rocked Swackard to the core. He and his team jumped in the car and sped off for Thomas' grandparents home, radioing the county office for backup.

CHAPTER 31

Thomas kept a keen eye on his uncle as Tyron floored the pedal to the floor. They were behind Miss Groovy and Mason in their vehicles, heading back for the epic showdown between Thomas, his father, and his grandparents. Pilo was fully awaken by now and he and Thomas shared their stories about their family members, Manny, and talks of horror and deceit. Thomas was eager to get in his father's face to confront him about the uncle he's been hiding and the aunt he viciously raped and murdered thirty-two years ago. The more they talked, the more angrier Thomas became. Anger turned to fear and panic as Thomas' anxiety worsened. Honestly, Thomas has been putting a front on for all of his family and friends. He never fully recovered from the past events that has happened in his life. He had a hard time dealing with the mental battles that played out in his head. Even when he tried to talk to his parents about it, they would just tell him that's it was nothing to worry about. Pray about it; go to church; talk to Rev. Jackson. Jackson was the last person he wanted to see. He vividly recalled Jackson telling his father years ago that Manny was 'possessed with the devil', that autism was a man-made disease so that the government can give kids medicine to control their minds. So Thomas took on more responsibilities that he could handle, only making his mental health worse. He put his head down, pretending to be sleep, and swallowed four 'Blue Diamond' pills he found stashed in his drawer after Skully destroyed the ones he had in the car in front of Chief's barber shop. Shortly after, he had drifted in sleep, welcoming the vivid nightmares and hallucinations the drugs brought on. Crash! Thomas was jolted out of his sleep as the back of Tyron's Escalade was hit! Turning around, Big T's heart sank, and horror filled his spirit at the sight behind him. It was the Crown Victoria with the faded top in hot pursuit! In the car were the two knuckleheads that tried to run him over, as well as the Haitian Sensation-Takeout, Augusten, Pierre, and Julien. *"Thomas, what's going on? Who's that behind us trying to run us off the road?"* inquired Tyron, who picked up the speed. Thomas explained to him that people were trying to kill him and his friends. Tyron instructed Ebony to take the wheel. After they exchanged places, they let down the back seats and moved Pilo up closer to the front. Tyron lifted the panel in his trunk and pulled out a shotgun. He jumped back up in the passenger seat and opened the window. *I'm gonna try to ward these assholes off! Keep an eye out for your uncle- better yet, Thomas you come drive and Ebony, get back there and look out for Mr. Pilo. Stay close to the floor as possible!"* Once again exchanging positions, Thomas looked out the rearview mirror as the driver of the Crown Vic approached closer to ram them. Tyron let off one shot, blowing out the right headlight of the Crown Vic. The car lost control for a moment, but then got back on its murderous path. Mason called Thomas. *"Big T, get into the other lane besides us. Skully and Bumble can use their heat along with Tyron to kill these muthafuckas before they kill us!"* Thomas agreed but he had to be very cautious. They were on a two lane road, and he had to be mindful of oncoming traffic. One wrong move and it was a head on collision for all of them! Thomas swerved to the other lane alongside Mason. Bumble let off a shot, which shot out the front passenger tire. The Crown Vic became uncontrollable. Skully switched places with Bumble and blew out the driver front tire. One last shot from Tyron blew out the windshield, sending the Crown Vic veering off the road into a ditch.

With one problem solved, the two cars got back into position, and headed towards their destination.

CHAPTER 32

The family and guests at Albert Senior and Dorris' house stood in utter disbelief as Robert was sent flying across the room, landing onto the drink table. *"Thomas! Thomas Darnell Jenkins, what the hell has become of you!?"*, yelled Della as Thomas laid a massive punch to his father's chest, followed by a hurl across the tented room. *"Liar! Rapist! Murder! You fucking piece of shit! How could you!"*, screamed Thomas. Robert managed to get himself off the table, only to see Thomas charging towards him like a bull. Thomas pummeled his father to the floor, punching him with all power in his hands. His male cousins pulled Thomas off of his father, demanding that he explain his disrespectful actions. Thomas and his friends pushed them away, then they turned their attention to Thomas' elderly grandparents. *"And you worthless bastards let him get away with it, convincing Detective McMasters to let one son take the blame for a murder that another son, my dad, actually did! And you proclaim to be Christians; to be loving; you've faked and fronted for all these years! It's time! Past time to tell the truth! About our family, about our secrets; about the dirty deeds you and Robert have done and covered up over the years. Your lives, your marriage, have all been a lie, a damn lie!"* Rape, murder, what was these people hiding was what the curious crowd of guest and clueless family members could only say, including Della. But Robert, his parents, and siblings knew, and they were silent, stoned-faced, emotionless. Suddenly, Jacob and Miss Groovy entered the tent, standing on either side of Pilo. The look of scorn on Pilo's face seemed to cut deep into Dorris, as she proceeded to cover her face. Robert began to sweat, clutching his chest, as if he was having a heart attack. Albert Senior sat emotionless, staring into the eyes of the son he discarded thirty-two years ago. Della could hardly contain her emotions. *"Pilo, is that....you.......is that really you? Oh my God what has happened to you? Where have you been all these years? I was told that you died in a mental hospital."* She ran up and gave her brother-in-law a great hug. Pilo returned the hug, and they both cried and cried. Thomas' other aunts and uncles were stunned at the presence of their brother, and began to shed tears themselves. *"Who is this, Big T?"*, asked one of his cousins. Thomas glared with evil intent and pointed at his grandparents. *"Why don't you ask them, and your uncle Robert, and your parents. They know exactly who this is. All of you need to burn in Hell for what you've done!"* The cousins looked at Thomas, then their parents and grandparents. None of them would speak, as they stared at Morris hanging onto his sister-in-law. Uncle Isaac shook his head. *"We didn't do anything, Thomas, I swear we had nothing to do with this. We were threatened not to ever speak about that fateful day-".* "Shut up! Just shut up!", scolded Jasmin. *"As children at that time, I understand your silence and fear of being punished, but as you became adults, you should have known better. You continued to live your lives while your brother was fighting to keep his!"* Pilo looked at his parents. *" I don't know you anymore, and I don't ever want to get to know you. Take a look at me- the damage you have caused; the injustice you dealt to me, Albert Jr. Gloria, Isaac, Patricia, and most importantly, Miranda. She was my sister- your flesh and blood- and she didn't deserve to die at the hands of a satanic spirit whom you cherished more than God himself!"* Just then, Robert approached his brother. *" Bastard, I should have killed you that night too when I had the chance! Miranda was a reject, a pain, a mental retard ,a burden, like Mama and Daddy used to tell me. She was sucking the life out of them! Her psychological issues, her seizures, her many health problems. It was always something wrong with her! We had to always take care and pay attention to her! She was sucking the life and the money out of our parents, and I wasn't going to stand around and let that happen! I was going to be the star of the family, the one that got the recognition, the fame for my basketball talent, not you. You should have never gotten the glory that I deserved growing up! I never intended to rape her, but after Della's parents weren't home to bring her over here, I figured I'd lose my virginity the best way I knew how."* Della cringed at the words her husband uttered. *"Robert, you are a sick, heartless, cruel, evil person. I never knew this depth of hatred you had for Miranda. I know you got impatient with her at times, but I never imagined that you would rape and kill your own sister. You are sickening beyond words, and definitely not the man I fell in love with as a* teen. *You've hidden your demons very well, fooling just about everyone around you!"* She turned to her in-laws and lashed out at them, blaming them for their family's dysfunction. Dorris shrugged her shoulders. *"The way Miranda was, maybe she's better off dead and gone anyways",* she sneered. Albert Senior nodded in agreement, looking at Pilo. *"At least your mother and I called every week to get an update on you. That Dr. Bhamra and Myrtice, I think that's her name, would always tell us how unruly you were. We told them to keep you injected with medications, hoping they would erase your memory-"* *"Dad, mom, how dare you treat Morris like this? It's like you wanted him to die!"* said Patricia as she, Isaac, and Albert Junior got into a verbal argument with their parents. The atmosphere became hostile. Everyone in the room was enraged at the revelation of the Jenkins' family secrets. Pilo never took his eyes on his other adversary- Robert. *" You weak, pathetic fool, you'd never be able to overpower me, with all those drugs in your system-ever!"*, snorted Robert as he and Pilo squared up against each other. *"No, Uncle can't beat your ass now, but I sure can, and I will, Robert!"*, yelled Thomas, cutting in front of his uncle. Robert laid a fist in his son's face, knocking Thomas to the ground. Della and Jasmin yelled for the father and son to stop, but to no avail. Thomas tackled his father to the ground and they both laid punches to each other. Thomas eventually overpowered his father, and began to wrap his massive hands around Robert's neck. As Robert struggled to breathe, he began to foam at the mouth. Bumble, Mason, Skully, Noble, and Jacob pulled Thomas off of his dad. *"He's not worth losing your life over, he's not worth killing"*, they all reiterated to Thomas, attempting to quell his rage. Thomas stopped and looked around- his life, his entire family, was in shambles. He looked at Pilo screaming at his parents and siblings; the guests were arguing and fighting amongst themselves, and he spotted his mom, Jasmin, Ebony, and Miss Groovy in the corner crying. As he began to ponder on the one thing that was missing, he heard someone yell out! It was Brenda, Tawny's mother, and she'd burst into the tent. *"Oh my God, oh my God. Thomas, boys, come out here quick. Some men just pulled up here, went and grabbed a little boy out of the house, and they have a rope around his neck!"*

CHAPTER 33

Hysteria hit the chaotic scene as Thomas heard the wailing screams of his brother Manny. He, along with his friends and Jacob, bolted out of the tent. *"Oh shit! It's Chief and Baptiste, and they got Manny's neck tied to a rope!"*, shouted Bumble as he sprinted towards them. Big T and the other boys followed Bumble in pursuit, determined to kill Chief and Baptiste dead. During the family breakdown in the tent, Baptiste, Chief, the Haitian Sensation, and the goons that tried to run over Big T and Bumble, arrived at Albert Senior and Dorris' house. Baptiste was familiar with the house, as he came here many summers when he was a child with his good friend, Robert. They had burst into the house, where John, Matt, and Brenda were keeping watch over Manny, who was asleep in his aunt Miranda's room. They overpowered John and Matt, taking Manny hostage. Brenda managed to hide until they left, and she was able to run out and get Thomas. Big T, Mason, Skully, Noble, and Jacob jumped over the rock fence, only to be face to face with the Haitian and Peak Ridge thugs. Takeout imprinted his brass knuckles to Big T's face, stunning the star basketball player. *"Who's going to be the star ball player now, punk!"*, laughed Takeout as he, Pierre, Julien, and Augusten beat him to a pulp. Chief had brought some of his henchmen for backup, and they managed to get a hold of Noble, Mason, Skully, and Jacob. Bumble, who had ran way ahead of the group, was struggling to get Manny away from Chief and Baptiste. Bumble yelled for help, but all of his friends were pinned down by the thugs. By this time, the Haitian sensation had a noose around Thomas' neck. He saw Jasmin and Della run out to help Bumble. Manny eventually freed himself from Baptiste's grip and started running. Jasmin,

Della, and Bumble valiantly fought Baptiste and Chief, but the two men were too powerful. Chief slapped Jasmin, picked her up, and threw her at a great distance towards the like he was throwing a ball, while Baptiste had grabbed Della by her hair and slammed her into the grass. Thomas' rage roared inside of him, and the spirit of God and Ogun themselves empowered him to take over his adversaries. He pushed the Haitian Sensation off of him and ran towards Chief and Baptiste. As he was going towards them, John and Matt emerged out of nowhere, along with the assistance of Lieutenant Swackard, McArthur, and the two troopers. They courageously fought Chief's henchmen, and the Middleton High school original players and Jacob ran down to help Thomas. As the five boys battled Chief and Baptiste, Thomas helped his mother and Jasmine to their feet. *"Go back in the tent now!"* yelled Big T. *"B-b-b-but, you have have a noose around your neck baby"*, stuttered Jasmin. *" Let me help you take it off"*, insisted Della. Big T would not budge. *"I'm not worried about that right now, I'm worried about you! Get back in the tent now! These guys ain't playing! They're trying to kill me, and they will kill you too! Get in the damn tent now!"* Della and Jasmin reluctantly ran back. Confused, Thomas looked around and around. His head was spinning, and he was feeling the effects of the drugs he'd taken earlier. Then suddenly, he felt the noose getting tighter around his neck. He was instantly jerked backwards, hitting his head on a rock. As he looked up, he saw the soulless, hollow eyes of his father standing above him. Thomas knew what this moment was coming down to- his father was trying to kill him!

CHAPTER 34

"Look at you, so-called hero. Well tonight, you're gonna be a matyr, at the hands of the one that helped bring you on this fucking piece of dirt called Earth! Pathetic, a waste of human life, just like your retarded ass brother Manny. Fuck both of you, especially you", Robert snickered. While Thomas' comrades were still in battle with his enemies, Robert tugged at the noose and began to drag Thomas to the oak tree that the kids all swung from during their summer outings. Thomas couldn't utter a sound; the rope was too tight around his neck. He was gasping for air, struggling to breathe. His chest was tight, and his eyes were watery. They got near the oak tree when Thomas looked out of the left corner of his eye. *"There ain't gonna be no martyr, just a dead, worthless muthafucka, and that muthafucka is you! Get yo' got damn hands off my nephew!"* Pilo

pummeled Robert into the tree, and the two brothers wrangled with each other. *"I'm the one that should have killed you, years before you killed our sister!"*, yelled Pilo as he took a rock and pounded Robert's face with it. *"I see you still have the battle scars Miranda scratched in your face. I'm glad you're able to look in the mirror everyday, as it reminds you of your horrible sins!"*. Thomas jumped out of the brothers' way. He looked down the lakeshore, and his heart sank! Manny was running towards the dock, trying to get into the water! Thomas yelled Manny's name. *"Manny, Manny, stop! Don't go into the water. Hold on brother, I'm coming, I'm coming!"*. Thomas hurriedly raced towards the dock to save his brother. His head was bleeding profusely from the injury he sustained on the rock. He felt himself blacking out, but he knew he had to keep pushing. He stumbled, but he got back up. He felt the pain from his right knee, but Big T kept running. His fear turned up several notches as he watched Manny climb the rope ladder to the dock. Thomas tripped over another rock and fell, landing face first in the grass. He was tired, worn out, defeated. He couldn't go on any further. He just laid there, wanting life as he knew it to be over. He suddenly felt someone touch his shoulder. He looked up, but no one was near him. His mother and Jasmin were miles away, yelling for Manny to stop, yelling for him to get Manny off the dock. Big T struggled, but he managed to get himself up and continue his run towards his brother. As he was running, he kept feeling someone push him. He kept looking around, but no one was there. He didn't understand what was going on, but he couldn't think about it at that time. He'd finally neared the tall dock, but Manny was already up top. As Thomas began to climb, he felt the noose tugging around his neck. *"Not today, son not today! You're gonna die first! You let out all my secrets, and if I die, I'm taking your ass along with me!"*, Robert growled, yanking Thomas off the ladder. Father and son fought again, with Thomas pleading for his father to stop. *"Stop Robert, just leave me, mom, and Manny alone! You never loved us, you never cared for us. Just leave us be, and go on with your pathetic life."* Robert ignored him as he continually dragged his son. Thomas saw something shine amongst the grass. He picked up the glass shard in one and and gripped the ground with the other. He got up and cut Robert's arm with the glass piece. Robert yelled in pain as Robert ran back to the dock and climbed the ladder. There stood Manny, looking at the sunrise shining on the beautiful, peaceful waters. Thomas dragged himself to his brother. *"Manny, stay right there! Don't jump over, okay. Please, don't make another move!"* Manny turned around, and started walking towards his brother. He smiled and kept repeating *"water, water, water"* to Thomas. *"Yes Manny, we'll go swimming together tomorrow, but not right now. Then we'll go to Freida's for some ice cream afterwards, okay. I promise Manny, I promise."* Suddenly, Manny's smile melted away as he turned around and ran towards the end of the dock. *"No, no, noooooo!"*, Thomas yelled as he ran towards his brother. Manny stood at the edge of the dock, contemplating his next move. As Thomas reached out to grab his brother, Manny jumped up in the air and off the dock towards the lake. Thomas grabbed Manny by the collar of his shirt. In an instant, a bright, beautiful light flashed before his eyes. Thomas gazed at the streets of gold and a silhouette of someone he didn't recognize. Thomas could hear the harps of Heaven playing beautiful music. He heard Jasmin and Della screaming. He heard the pleas from his aunts, uncles and cousins telling someone to stop! He felt the noose tug at his neck again, but then its grip loosened. He felt pain from the right side of his head, but that quickly dissipated as he looked up to a beautiful, fiery halo encircling his being. Whether Thomas felt the three gunshots to his head or not remains to be seen. All Big T knew was that he felt at peace, he felt a calm spirit in his body. And he planted a smile on his face as he fell off the dock, splashing in the calm waters of the lake, with the noose still around his neck. He still had Manny by the collar of his neck, and he was determined to not let go.

Under the lake went Thomas and Manny. Although the waters were murky, Thomas could still see the bright, fiery halo around his face. Those streets of gold entered into his vision once again, and this time, he could make out what the silhouette was. A little girl, maybe eleven, maybe twelve, sat in the streets, twirling her long pigtails. Her big, beautiful brown eyes shined like real diamonds, not the 'Blue Diamonds' Thomas had been abusing for years. She motioned for Manny and Thomas to come to her. *"Come play with me Big T, please come play with me. Robert never wanted to play with me. All he wanted to do was hurt me. But not you- you're not like your mean old daddy! He did a very bad thing to me, but it's okay now. I live in a big ol house now where Robert and mommy and daddy and those mean, bad doctors can't hurt me anymore. Come stay here with me, so Robert won't do anymore bad things to you either. And Manny? He can come with us another time. He can't leave your mommy and your friends just yet. They need him a lot more right now. I didn't have any friends down there, and I want you to be my friend up here. Will you be my friend up here? Please, Thomas, please?"* Thomas' smile grew bigger than ever. Life with his aunt Miranda on the golden streets had to be a far cry from the crazy streets of Dover, Delaware. Miranda placed angel wings on Manny. *"Okay Manny, you can fly away now. Go back to Aunt Della, but stay away from Robert. He's a mean man! Don't let him hurt you like he hurt me and your brother! Come on Thomas, it's time to go!"* She took Big T by the hand and they walked away, away into her big ol' house. Manny floated back to the surface of the water, while Thomas' spirit floated high unto the Heavens.

CHAPTER 35

The chauffeur took Della back to her apartment above Freida's Ice Cream and Treats. Della couldn't drive anymore, and she hired a personal chauffeur to drive her around. Two years after Thomas's death and funeral she was still overwhelmingly emotional, and she just wanted to get some sleep. The chauffeur helped Della climb the steps and into her place. After taking a shower, she settled in bed, trying to take a nap, but she couldn't sleep. She called her very good friend, Freida. She and Freida had been friends since Della's family took Freida's family in years ago when they first arrived in the States from Jamaica. Della's father let Freida's family borrow money to start their restaurant. And they have remained close for all these years. The door knocked; Della let Freida in and they embraced. "I know I need to rest but right now I need a huge favor", said Della. "Anything for you, my friend", responded Freida in her thick, Jamaican accent. After discussing her plans, Freida and Della jumped into the car and drove off. On their way to their destination, Della reflected on her life and how her world has been turned upside down. Manny was now in a children's home care system about thirty miles away from Dover. Manny had been in the water too long with Thomas and nearly drowned. The lack of oxygen going to his brain brought on further damage, and now Manny was in a vegetative state. He'd still smile and blinked his eyes as Della, Jasmin, Bumble, Noble, Skully, Mason, and his home school teacher shared fond memories of his brother, but he couldn't talk at all. Maybe one day, he'll be able to talk again, Della said to herself. After finding about her husband's infidelity, Della dismissed Jayla. Jayla eventually moved far away; Della wasn't sure, but she didn't give a damn. Dr. Crumbly still practiced and would drop by from time to time. She cut off all communication to her in-laws, as well as Albert Jr., Isaac, Patricia, and Gloria. Lieutenant Swackard, State Trooper McArthur, and two other officers were charged with tampering with evidence and aiding and abetting two criminals. Swackard received fifteen years in prison while the other were given seven years. Jacob's in school now to become a nurse after getting clearance from the Delaware Board of Nursing. Authorities could never find any clear evidence that he and Miss Groovy stole medical records from the mental hospital; maybe Swackard had something to do with that. Tyron and the other male nurse faced disciplinary infractions against them, but they still remain nurses at different locations. Healing Minds Mental Institute was shut down after the evidence Jacob and Miss Groovy uncovered landed in the hands of a New York Times reporter. The fiasco behind Miranda's death and the jailing of an innocent teenager drove the main detective-turned Senator, McMasters, to commit suicide days before he was to be arrested. Drs. Bhamra and Negron received life sentences in federal prison for their crimes, while Myrtice received forty years for unlawfully practicing nursing without a license. Her misdeeds, come to find out, caused four deaths of patients at the mental hospital. Big Rich, Sheldon, and Gunner each got ten years for their role in the abuse of Morris aka Pilo, as well as other patients. Brenda was finally reunited with her daughter Tawny, but the pressures of life were too much for her to handle. She committed suicide six months after Big T's death. Miss Groovy and her husband John still live in Dover. They try to keep a low profile, although they do get out to see Jacob and Manny from time to time. Matt still works as a computer engineer. Ebony and Tryon divorced soon the events of the night of the escape, but she still keeps in contact with Della and the others. Bumble, Noble, Skully, and Mason all are in college on scholarship and excelling academically. Jasmin, still shook up from Thomas' death, took a break after high school. Della prayed daily that Jasmin would eventually pull herself together; Thomas would not have wanted her to be moping over his passing. And Robert? After the real story was told on Miranda's death, he was charged with rape and murder, but the charges were dropped by the new district attorney that was elected a year after he was charged. He'd collected half of the life insurance policy on Thomas' death, and got him and his parents far away from Delaware. Della divorced him, wanting nothing but her freedom from that monster. Rumor were going around that Robert and Jayla were living together, but Della wasn't so sure. Della and Freida finally arrived at their destination. They walked into the room and spotted Morris 'Pilo' Jenkins tending to his flowers and tomatoes. Her brother-in-law looked like a real live human being now. All charged were dropped against him and he was freed by the state. He received compensation from a lawsuit against the state of Delaware and was now living in a halfway house, which was his choosing. He needed to be here to adjust back to life; he hadn't seen the outside walls of his prison cell for thirty-two years. Della gave Pilo a hug and gave him two baskets full of goodies. He sat down and opened up the baskets. He pulled out two newspapers and magazines that didn't come out in the last century. He looked up at his caring sister-in-law and gave her a thumbs up, chowing down on the four grilled cheese sandwiches and tomato soup Freida made for him.

THE AUTHOR

Sarah Carmele McGriff came into this world in the great year of 1980, and her life has been a whirlwind of adventure ever since. Sarah loves books, and has been an avid reader since her school-age years. Writing has always been in her soul; but she never imagined that it would take her to the position that she is in now.

Caring for others has always been Sarah's passion, as her mother was a nurse. Sarah started her career as a Certified Nursing Assistant, moving up to become a Licensed Practical Nurse, and now a Registered Nurse.

Sarah finally decided to step out on faith, gathered her thoughts, conquered her fears, and prayed to God to allow her to be a vessel to write her first book. In addition to writing, Sarah loves to read, go to the beach, and draw and sketch on occasions. Sarah eventually wants to step into the movie production world. Sarah aspires to become a screenwriter as well as a movie director. Sarah currently resides in Florida with her two children and her Shih Tzu, Jim Brown AKA Brownie.